Garrett couldn't deny Lexie.

He opened his mouth to tell her, but that was as far as he got. He saw the movement out of the corner of his eye. Behind her. To the right of the double French doors that led to his backyard.

"Get down," Garrett said. He practically whispered it, but it still came through loud and clear like an order.

Lexie tried to follow his gaze, no doubt to see what had triggered his reaction, but he didn't give her a chance. He slapped off the light switch, plunging them into darkness. In the same motion, he hooked his arm around her waist and shoved her to the floor. It was barely in time.

Because a bullet slammed through one of the French doors, pelting them with a deadly spray of splintered wood and broken glass....

DELORES FOSSEN

THE CRADLE FILES

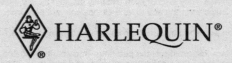

HARLEQUIN®

TORONTO • NEW YORK • LONDON
AMSTERDAM • PARIS • SYDNEY • HAMBURG
STOCKHOLM • ATHENS • TOKYO • MILAN • MADRID
PRAGUE • WARSAW • BUDAPEST • AUCKLAND

ISBN-13: 978-0-373-22932-1
ISBN-10:   0-373-22932-1

THE CRADLE FILES

ABOUT THE AUTHOR

Imagine a family tree that includes Texas cowboys, Choctaw and Cherokee Indians, a Louisiana pirate and a Scottish rebel who battled side by side with William Wallace. With ancestors like that, it's easy to understand why Texas author and former U.S. Air Force captain Delores Fossen feels as if she was genetically predisposed to writing romances. Along the way to fulfilling her DNA destiny, Delores married a U.S. Air Force Top Gun, who just happens to be of Viking descent. With all those romantic bases covered, she doesn't have to look too far for inspiration.

Books by Delores Fossen

HARLEQUIN INTRIGUE

CAST OF CHARACTERS

Sergeant Garrett O'Malley—A bad-boy San Antonio cop with something to prove to himself and his high-achieving family. But his plans and his life take a dangerous turn when Lexie Rayburn, his former lover, returns with news that someone has stolen their newborn baby.

Lexie Rayburn—A ruthless doctor stole her baby minutes after she gave birth, and the doctor's attempt to kill Lexie has robbed her of vital memories. But she has no trouble remembering the attraction she feels for Garrett. Unfortunately, a relationship with Garrett could cost him his badge and their lives.

Billy Avery—Lexie's former boss who's now behind bars awaiting appeal of a felony conviction. Would he have taken Lexie and Garrett's baby as leverage to prevent Lexie from testifying against him if he's granted a new trial?

Dr. Linnay Blake—Director of the clinic where the baby was stolen. Dr. Blake could be merely a scapegoat for the real kidnapper, or she could be behind a sinister plot to provide stolen babies to unsuspecting adoptive parents.

Alicia Peralta—The clinic nurse who tries to help Garrett and Lexie find their child. Are Alicia's motives pure, or is she trying to steer them away from her own criminal activities?

Dr. Andrew Darnell—He's the obstetrician Lexie believes tried to kill her. Unfortunately, there's no proof, and with Lexie's broken memories, the police have little to go on.

Irving Kent—Dr. Darnell's attorney and the man linked to many suspicious adoptions. Is he responsible for the disappearance of Lexie and Garrett's child?

Chapter One

With water snaking down his body, Sergeant Garrett O'Malley headed toward the laundry room in search of a clean towel—something he wished he'd done *before* his shower. He only made it a step outside the steamy bathroom when he realized he wasn't alone.

There was a shadowy figure standing at the other end of the dark hall.

Adrenaline knifed through him, and his heartbeat went into overdrive. He made a split-second assessment to make sure it wasn't a family member. It wasn't. And he automatically reached for his weapon, which obviously wasn't there, since he didn't have on a stitch of clothes.

He cursed.

Because that's when he noticed the intruder was armed.

"Don't move," she said in a hoarse whisper.

She. It was definitely a female. Garrett didn't hear enough of her voice, though, to recognize it. It was the same for the woman herself. She stayed in the darkness, her face and body hidden.

Well, if this was a robbery, she'd picked a good time for it. He was not only towel-less, he was totally unprepared. Garrett's mind raced with questions. What did she want, and how the devil had she gotten in?

And did she have plans to kill him?

His cop's brain immediately went to work, and within seconds he decided this wasn't a good time for an all-out fight.

Not with her pointing that gun straight at him.

If he couldn't talk her into surrendering her weapon, his best move would be to make a dive for his bedroom—where he'd left his loaded 9 mm, standard issue Glock on his dresser. Thankfully, his bedroom and that Glock were only about eight feet away, and the door was wide open.

Of course, being buck naked didn't help.

And the dive onto the hardwood floor would hurt like crazy, but it was better than getting shot. He'd been there, done that, not once but twice, and he didn't want to repeat the ordeal anytime soon.

"Who are you, and why are you here?" Garrett demanded while he calculated the best moment to disarm her or to begin that dive. If he could somehow distract her, that would help.

But he immediately rethought the idea.

Since she'd broken into the home of a cop and was holding him at gunpoint, she probably wasn't the distractible type. *If* she knew he was a cop, that was. Maybe this was a random burglary. That didn't make the situation any less dangerous. In fact, the stakes might escalate if she discovered who he really was. She might try to kill him just so she could eliminate a witness.

She stepped closer, toward the milky-yellow light that spilled out from the bathroom. Her cautious footsteps barely made a sound. But her breathing sure did. It was coming out in rough, hurried gusts.

"I need to talk to you," she said.

Garrett froze and put his Glock-retrieving plan on hold. Now he recognized that voice, and it set off all kinds of alarms in his head.

Not good alarms, either.

"Lexie?" he asked. "Is that you?"

She froze. For a few moments. And then she inched closer still. She stared at him and squinted, as if trying to peer through the darkness for a good look. Garrett did the same.

Yep. It was Lexie Rayburn all right, though he'd never seen her wear her hair that long or in that particular style. Her straight rust-colored locks fell choppy, loose and disheveled onto her shoulders.

The last time he'd seen her, she'd been cursing a blue streak and had thrown her panties at him. Well, maybe not *at* him, exactly, but in his general direction.

He was lucky she hadn't thrown something heavier and more lethal.

That throwing incident was... When? A few months shy of a year ago, when Lexie had walked out of his life. But she hadn't just *walked out*. She'd left him with a lot of questions, no answers, and she'd put his badge on the line. Since his badge was the most important thing in his life, that had not sat well with him.

It still didn't.

Garrett's jaw tightened.

She moved even closer, and he got a better look at her gun. An RG .22, commonly referred to as a Saturday Night Special. Another surprise. The cheap, no-frills weapon wasn't her usual choice of firearms, but then neither were the clothes. She wore loose faded jeans, scuffed Doc Martens and a baggy navy-blue flannel shirt that was frayed at the cuffs. It was at least two sizes too big and practically swallowed her.

"Garrett O'Malley?" she asked.

And it was definitely a question. No doubt Lexie's version of sarcasm.

Oh, this was going to get messy.

He just stared at her.

"Are you Garrett O'Malley?" she pressed.

Riled at her dry-as-dust sarcasm, at the gun and at the woman herself, he opened his arms. "You tell me. You're not seeing anything you haven't seen before."

He'd meant his remark to sting, a reminder that he'd been her one-night stand. Her choice. Not his.

She took his remark as an invitation. Her gaze combed over him, starting at his face. Her marine-blue eyes met his green ones. Briefly. And then she slid that gaze all the way past his bare chest and stomach to his equally bare groin.

Her eyes paused.

Considerably.

For a long time.

Normally, he wouldn't have been so bothered by the close scrutinization from a lover, former or otherwise, but these obviously weren't normal circumstances.

"Mind telling me why you're here and what your plans are for that gun?" he insisted.

She nodded. Not a confident I'm-in-charge-here nod, either. It was shaky. In fact, there was something shaky about her entire demeanor. "I want answers."

So, this was maybe a payback visit in order to rehash their last encounter. A blast from the past. Lucky him. "I don't know the questions, but I have a few of my own. For starters, how did you get into my house?" Because he knew for a fact she didn't have a key.

She tipped her head toward the kitchen. "The patio door. You left it unlocked when you took out the trash after you got home from work."

Hell's bells. Not the brightest move he could have made, especially for a cop. He'd made that little faux pas only about fifteen minutes ago, which meant she hadn't waited too long to confront him. Maybe she'd delayed her entrance until he got in the shower so she could catch him when he wasn't near his Glock. Or perhaps she'd waited until he was what polite company would call *indisposed*.

She'd succeeded.

He was as indisposed as he could get. Still, that theory only created more questions.

"Why the gun?" he asked.

She glanced at it and swallowed hard. "I wasn't sure I could trust you."

"You can't." And that was a sore spot for him. Even now. "But then, I obviously can't trust you, either. Still, a gun? Judas Priest, Lexie. That's a little over the top, even for you."

Her forehead bunched up. "I wanted to make sure you listened to what I had to say."

"Oh, I'm listening. Pardon the pun, but I'm all ears." Garrett turned toward his bedroom, but then stopped and looked at her. Actually, he glared. And he knew his glare was a winner. That particular facial expression alone had gotten perps to surrender. "I'm going to get dressed now, and I'd rather you didn't try to kill me while I do that, okay?"

He didn't wait for her to respond or concur with his smart-mouth challenge. Figuring that Lexie wouldn't shoot him in the back, Garrett headed to his bedroom.

"Wait a minute," she snarled. She hurried after him, but then stopped in the doorway. "Don't just walk away from me. I'm holding you at gunpoint."

"Believe me, I'm aware of that. Call me old-fashioned, but I'd rather not have this conversation or try to wrestle that .22 away from you while I'm buck naked. And make no mistake about it—I *am* going to wrestle that gun away from you if you don't come to your senses."

Besides, if this did turn into a wrestling match or even more, Garrett didn't want his fellow peace officers to show up and find him wearing only his birthday suit and a glare. There had already been enough rumors and career-damaging innuendos as it was. He didn't want to add this to the record, even if seeing Lexie brought back memories.

Both bad and good—and very, very good ones.

Riled not only at Lexie, but at himself and his too vivid, lust-induced reminiscence, Garrett grabbed a pair of Wranglers from the floor and slipped them on. Not easily. His still-soaking-wet body caused the denim to drag, catch and cling. Worse, it dragged, caught and clung while Lexie gawked at the entire awkward, semihumiliating process.

He didn't let her gawking deter him, though. He zipped them up—carefully, since he wasn't wearing underwear—while he also checked the position of his Glock. He didn't relish the idea of drawing that gun on Lexie, but it was obvious she had a bone to pick with him. He didn't want that bone-picking argument to turn into shots being fired.

Ironic.

Because he'd never thought of Lexie as dangerous. Armed, yes. Capable of kicking butt. But not lethal in a criminal, out-of-control sort of way. He was obviously wrong. Any woman who would pull a gun on him so they could *talk* had gone a few steps past that dangerous level and was definitely out of control.

What was wrong with her, anyway?

Yes, she had a right to be riled. But, heck, so did he. More so than she obviously was. Yet Lexie seemed to be putting all the blame on him.

"You didn't wait around for the trial to end," Garrett said, figuring his words would hit a few raw nerves. Because she hadn't waited around for a lot of things—like to finish her testimony. Or even to say goodbye. "But I guess you know your former boss was convicted on all charges and is behind bars?"

"William Avery," she said.

"William?" Garrett repeated. He stared at her. Well now, that confirmed something was truly wrong. Lexie always called her former boss Billy.

"I read about William, and you, on the Internet," she continued. "That's how I knew you were a cop. That's how I figured out where to find you."

Yet more confirmation that something was wrong. Lexie knew he was a cop, and she darn sure knew where to find him. "Are you okay?"

A soft burst of air left her mouth. Almost a laugh, but there was no humor in it. Her voice was laced with fatigue and sarcasm when she admitted, "No. I'm not okay." And she left her somewhat lame explanation at that.

"Did Billy's...William's *friends* threaten you or something?" It might explain why she was here. Maybe she'd come because Garrett was a cop. However, that was a stretch. There were a lot of cops in San Antonio, and he was almost certainly the last one she'd ask for help.

"Maybe," she mumbled, as if she were considering that for the first time. "I don't know if he's behind this or not. But I don't think so."

Her voice cracked on the last word, and she blinked back tears.

Actual tears.

All right. That took a chunk out of the Texas-size chip Garrett carried on his shoulder. Here, he wanted nothing more than to tell Lexie that her untimely departure had not only left him in departmental hot water, it'd also put a few fractures in his desires to get involved in another relationship—ever. But Garrett put his own issues and old grudges on the back burner. After what she'd done to him, he didn't care much for Lexie. In fact, what he felt for her fell into the *strongly dislike* category, but it was obvious she was in trouble. Unfortunately, that and the tears brought out protective instincts that he knew he stood no chance of suppressing.

Still, he'd try. Hard.

Because, after all, this was Lexie. He wasn't ready to go a second round with her. The sooner he could get her out of his life, the better.

"Other than the veiled threats he made to you during the trial, I haven't heard anything from Billy Avery," he tried to assure her, while he calculated how he was going to subdue her so he could confiscate that gun. "In fact, he's been a model prisoner. Probably because he's hoping to have the murder and racketeering verdicts overturned on appeal." With that, Garrett paused. Rethought. "He threatened you so you wouldn't testify against him if he was granted a new trial?"

Lexie shook her head and left the doorway. She stepped warily into the room, her gaze darting around as if she expected someone to jump out from the corners. "I haven't spoken to Billy Avery."

Garrett believed her, especially since prison authorities would have alerted someone in the SAPD if Lexie had phoned or shown up at the prison. But believing her on that specific point didn't help clear up everything else.

"Look, I could stand here and try to guess what's wrong," he stated, "but wouldn't it be easier if you just told me what this is all about?"

She looked at him as if trying to decide what to say. Or what not to say. Finally, she nodded. Then nodded again. "Someone tried to kill me."

Whoa. That got his attention. "Who?"

But he was already fairly sure of the answer. If someone had tried to kill her, then Billy Avery or one of his *associates* was likely behind it. That was the reason the cops and the feds had wanted Lexie in the Witness Protection Program. A program she'd declined by simply leaving and not telling anyone, including Garrett, her whereabouts.

He hadn't thought for a minute that she was dead, either. She was too resourceful for that. So over the past months he had come to accept that she'd disappeared because of him. Their little encounter had nearly cost the state a guilty verdict for Billy Avery, and it'd nearly cost Garrett his badge. The flack hadn't stopped there. His brother and sister, both fellow cops, had had their own sterling careers tarnished by standing up for him.

No. Garrett wouldn't forget the mess Lexie had made of his life and the trouble she'd caused for his family.

"I don't know who tried to kill me," she said. "But that's not the reason I came here." Lexie plowed the fingers of her left hand through her hair and scooped it away from her face. It didn't help. The loose strands simply fell back into place. "I need to ask you something, something personal, and I want the truth."

Garrett waited. And waited. But she didn't finish her request for information. She just stood there, tears threatening and her bottom lip trembling. He forced himself to stay put. Comforting could lead to holding.

Or shooting.

Neither was going to happen, not tonight. Not ever.

"You need to know what?" he pressed. "I'm not a mind reader, Lexie."

Without breaking eye contact, and without lowering her gun, she sat down on the foot of his bed. The mattress creaked softly.

She pulled in a long, weary breath, released it. "Are you the father of my baby?"

Chapter Two

"Am I what?" Garrett O'Malley demanded.

But he didn't just demand it. His hands went to his hips, and he pinned his Celtic-green gaze on her. With that stare, he questioned her integrity. Her presence.

And her sanity.

Lexie was right there with him. She, too, was questioning a lot of things, her sanity included. It was probably a huge mistake to come here like this, but she hadn't had a choice. She needed answers, and Sergeant Garrett O'Malley was the person most likely to have them.

Not exactly a comforting thought.

It was obvious that he hated her. Why, she didn't know. But from the few things she'd learned, he probably had good reason to. It was possible she had reasons to hate him as well.

"I asked if you're the father of my baby," Lexie clarified, though she was certain he'd heard her.

Hearing and grasping, however, were two different things. She'd basically just delivered a bomb-shell and was giving Garrett O'Malley mere seconds to absorb it. Heck, she'd had days and hadn't fully managed to, and what she *had* managed to under-stand, she didn't like.

She was in a lot of trouble.

But then, perhaps, so was Garrett.

She'd save that news for later. First, there was the issue of paternity.

"Well?" she prompted.

Lexie saw the moment that her bombshell actually registered. His eyes widened. Every muscle in his body seemed to turn to iron.

"Oh, man." He groaned and stepped back, his chest pumping as if he were suddenly starved for air. "Was that an honest-to-goodness question?"

"Unfortunately, yes." And she tried to brace herself for an equally honest answer. He held her life, her heart and her future in his hands, and he didn't even know it.

Yet.

He opened his mouth. Closed it. Only to open it again so he could curse. "Why are you doing this?"

She ignored his question. "Did we sleep together?"

"No." He said it without a shred of hesitation.

Lexie's heart sank to her knees. Oh, mercy. Had she gotten this all wrong?

Garrett let that unhesitant *no* bristle between them while he stared daggers at her. His mouth tightened into a semi-sneer. "But we did have sex," he clarified. "You left before either of us could get any *sleep.*"

The relief flooded through her. Why, she didn't know. Other than the fact O'Malley was a cop, he didn't seem like the best choice for fatherhood or a likely candidate to help keep her alive. From what she'd read about him, he had a penchant for attracting trouble. That penchant apparently included attracting her, as well.

"So, we weren't in love or anything like that?" she questioned.

"No." He practically spat out the word. More profanity followed. "If you want to put a label on it, we were in brief, temporary lust."

Yes. She could see that. Garrett O'Malley was, well, hot by anyone's standards.

Especially hers.

Even with the fatigue and the relentless haze in her brain, she couldn't deny that. He was lean and lethal, just over six feet tall, with a body and face that had probably garnered him many invitations to women's beds. Not exactly the knight in shining armor type with those jeans that clung to every part of him.

Heck, he wasn't even the cop type.

With that sopping wet, a-little-too-long, bronze-colored hair, hint of desperado stubble and bad boy demeanor, he would have been more at home on a Harley.

Or in a police lineup.

"Lust," Lexie mumbled. She'd counted on something more. Much more. Because she desperately needed his help. Still, lust would have to do, since it was all she had. "Did we have sex about nine and a half months ago?"

Oh, that riled him. She saw the anger flash in his eyes. It merged with the confusion and the profanity that was already there.

"You know we did." He stepped closer and aimed an accusing index finger at her. She wanted to get off the bed and move back. To keep her distance. But if she tried to stand up now, she'd risk falling flat on her face.

That would hardly be an effective bargaining position.

"So, what the hell is this all about?" he asked. "And while you're explaining, get to the part about me being the father of your baby. Are you actually saying you were pregnant?"

She considered her answer. There was only one way to go with this—she had to tell him the truth. Unfortunately, she wasn't sure just how much was true and how much was a product of the drug that'd been used to try to murder her.

"Let me start from the beginning." Lexie paused. "Or at least what I know to be the beginning. I haven't seen a doctor, but it seems as if I've, uh, lost some of my memory."

His accusing finger dropped slowly back to his

side, and even though his mouth didn't gape, it came close. "You have amnesia?"

She nodded. "Maybe."

"Maybe?"

Lexie tried not to huff at his sarcasm. They had too many battles ahead of them without him questioning everything she said. "*Maybe* is as good of an answer as I can give you right now. That's why I pawned my necklace and bought the gun. Because I didn't know if we were friends or enemies."

"There's a lot of gray area as far as our relationship is concerned. And some not so gray," he gruffly added. But the gruffness eased a bit when he continued. "You pawned your necklace—the gold rose with the diamond in the center?"

It was an odd question, but it also seemed important. She nodded. "Was the necklace a gift from you?"

"No. We didn't exchange gifts. Your father gave it to you. I'm just surprised you'd be willing to part with it."

She'd parted with it because she hadn't known its value, and because she'd needed money to survive. However, knowing now that her father had given it to her made her ache at losing something so precious.

Of course, she'd lost something else far more precious.

"Why don't we get back to your explanation?" Garrett insisted. "Approximately nine and a half months ago, we were together in a hotel room in downtown San Antonio."

"Having sex," she provided, latching on to the information as if it were nuggets of gold. Which in a way it was. Everything she could learn might bring her closer to unraveling this puzzle inside her head.

He confirmed that with a nod. "Afterward—"

She held up her hand. "Don't go there yet. Why was I in a hotel room with you having sex?"

The question earned her a blank stare. Hooking his thumbs into the waist of his jeans, Garrett leaned against the wall. "You honestly don't remember?"

"If I did, I wouldn't be asking. I'm not here to relive our past."

"Right. You're here because you want to know if I'm the father of your baby." More skepticism. Lexie totally understood his reaction. But she could also see that he was mentally doing the math. Nine and a half months ago fit with the other pieces of the puzzle.

She nodded. "And because someone tried to kill me."

His left eyebrow arched. Not exactly a vote of confidence. "Okay, I'll play. We were in a hotel room because you were in my protective custody. You were a material witness for your former boss, Billy Avery, and you testified against him for racketeering. Well, *partly* testified. You made it through the first day of questioning, but you left before you could finish."

"I was Billy Avery's bodyguard," she supplied.

He made a sound of agreement. "You remember that part, so your amnesia must be cured." More cynicism. Perhaps his way of coping. Or better yet, his way of tap-dancing around the other subject.

The baby.

"Not really," Lexie explained. "I read about it in the newspapers I found on the Internet." The images of those articles began to race through Lexie's head. She'd been having a lot of those lately. Unfocused thoughts. Blurry images. Lots and lots of confusion.

She didn't need the mental clutter now.

She had to focus.

"So, after I testified, we had sex…." Lexie almost had a *duh* moment and asked why again. But all she had to do was look at Garrett O'Malley and she knew the reason why. The lost memories hadn't dulled her physical reaction to this man. "Then, it's my guess something happened to cause me to leave?"

He didn't answer right away. "I think Avery's threats maybe got to you. You were scared."

She suspected he was omitting something important. "Anything else that might have contributed?"

"We argued." Just that. Tossed at her like a gauntlet. "Now, can we get to the baby part? If you have amnesia, how do you even know you had a child?"

Without loosening her grip on the gun, she caught her bulky shirt and lifted it so he could see the trio of pale, thready stretch marks on her stomach. "I think I remember going into labor three weeks and two days ago. That date is fixed in my head. I believe that's because the whole time I was in labor, I kept thinking that it would be my baby's birthday. But everything's jumbled. So, I could be wrong." A massive understatement, and it didn't apply just to her thought process but to her entire life. "Mercy, I know how all of this must sound."

"No. You don't. I step out of my shower, go in search of a towel and instead get held at gunpoint by an amnesiac woman who thinks I might be the father of her child. But the problem is, other than a few stretch marks, she's not even sure she had a baby."

Oh, Lexie was sure of that. Hard to forget the god-awful pain that had made her feel as if she were being ripped in two. And then, after hours and hours, the pain had stopped. She'd heard that soft, kitten-like cry. Even now, with all the uncertainty, that cry still got to her. That was her baby's cry, and no one could make her believe differently.

Grumbling something under his breath, Garrett walked closer, and closer, until he was practically looming over her. "Lexie, you need to put down that gun so I can take you to a doctor."

She frowned. She hadn't wanted the conversation to move in this direction. And she darn sure hadn't wanted him that near to her, either. "You mean a shrink? You don't believe the baby part."

He made a sound that could have meant

anything. Or nothing. "We only had sex once, and we used a condom."

Yet more unexpected information. She was getting a lot of that tonight. "Then something went wrong."

She tried to force her brain to remember exactly what. But it was useless. Forcing only seemed to make her memory cloudier.

Frustrated with herself she shook her head. His simultaneous movement registered just a second too late.

Garrett reached out.

Lightning fast.

And just like that, he snatched the gun from her hand.

He didn't stop there. In a little maneuver that was practically a blur, he came at her. Lexie turned, to try to scramble away from him, but Garrett practically tackled her. The momentum sent them both crashing onto the overly soft bed. He twisted his body to take the majority of the impact. But then he turned. Trapping her. So that she couldn't move.

Fighting through the initial panic, she took a moment to assess her situation. And it wasn't a very good assessment. Garrett was on top of her, his body completely covering hers. She was no longer armed.

But he was.

With her gun.

Even if he hadn't had a weapon in his right hand, his body would have certainly been classified as one. He was all sinew and muscle.

And he was all over her.

His right leg was wedged between hers. His chest squashed against her breasts. Their middles aligned perfectly, as if they were about to have sex.

That alignment didn't bring back any memories.

However, it did remind her that he was a very virile man.

As if she needed anything to remind her of *that*.

What was wrong with her, anyway? Her brain was messed up. So was her body. Only three and a half weeks ago she'd given birth, and here she was reacting to a man who for all practical purposes was a stranger. Maybe this was a bad case of postdelivery hormones. If so, it was a sick trick to play on her.

Because Garrett was so close, Lexie caught his scent. His ocean-scented deodorant soap. His shampoo. His spearmint toothpaste. And beneath all the toiletry stuff, his own scent was there. All man.

Not that she'd had any doubts about that.

"Well?" he said. Definitely not a question, but more like a challenge. It had a tinge of a Texas drawl and a hefty amount of anger in it.

He didn't believe her.

For the first time since she'd started this fiasco, Lexie was truly afraid. "What are you going to do to me?"

He blinked, surprised, as if genuinely insulted. "I'm not going to kill you, that's for sure. If I'd wanted you dead," he informed her, enunciating each word carefully, "you already would be."

Because she couldn't let him think she was weak, Lexie hiked up her chin and met him eye to eye. "I could say the same thing," she retorted.

Okay, so that was a lie. But maybe Garrett didn't know that, and right now, she'd do whatever it took, including an attempt at intimidation, to get his cooperation. She had to make him believe her because she needed his help.

He shifted slightly, so that his thigh wasn't pressed against the V junction of her jeans. "If the condom failed, then I have just one question," he said. "Where's the baby?"

It was the only question that mattered.

The memories of the delivery came flooding back. The pain. God, the pain. That tiny cry. And just like that, Lexie found herself blinking back more tears.

So much for her attempt at appearing strong and sturdy.

She was failing at a lot of things tonight.

"I tried to stop it," she heard herself say. Mercy, her voice was ripe with fatigue and weariness. "But the man was too strong."

Garrett eased off her. "The man who tried to kill you?"

"No. This man was there when I delivered. With the doctor. The doctor had slightly graying hair. He was tall, with wide shoulders. And he shoved a needle in my arm. It was filled with some kind of drug. I think it was the drug that left me with all these gaps in my memory."

Garrett stood, staring down at her. "Then how do you know the baby isn't a drug-induced figment?"

"She isn't a figment," Lexie insisted. "She's real."

Garrett paused. *"She?"*

"I didn't actually see the baby, but I'm positive it was a little girl."

His expression softened. Briefly. And then the concern returned and settled into his eyes. "Lexie, what happened? What did this man do?"

She wasn't even sure she could say the words aloud. Just thinking them nearly ripped her heart apart.

"He stole the baby. And we have to find her, Garrett. One way or another, we have to get our daughter back."

Chapter Three

Garrett felt as if someone had slugged him. Twice.

"Oh, man," he mumbled. And because he didn't know what else to say or do, he just stood there and kept mumbling it.

A baby.

Specifically, a three-and-a-half-week-old daughter.

A child he'd conceived with Lexie during the "adrenaline sex" they'd had after she testified against her boss.

Well, maybe.

And maybe all of this was some bizarre encounter with a woman who was no longer sane.

Except Lexie seemed sane. Well, she did if he disregarded half of what she'd said. Oh, and if he didn't count the fact that she'd broken into his house and held him at gunpoint.

Not exactly the actions of a sane woman.

But if what she'd told him was true, then what she had been through would have tested anyone's sanity.

Lexie got up from the bed. Not slowly, either. And she immediately started toward him.

"Don't you even think about trying to get this gun back," Garrett warned through clenched teeth. "And forget any thoughts about trying to pound me into the floor by using your martial arts training. And definitely don't do anything else that'll rile me."

She blinked. "I have martial arts training?"

He was certain he scowled—because under the circumstances it seemed a semi-trivial question and because he probably shouldn't have informed her of that particular talent. "Yeah. You do."

Lexie touched her fingertips to her right temple. "I wish I'd known that sooner."

"Lucky for me you didn't, because I obviously have enough to deal with." And he needed to start dealing. "Honesty time," he insisted, turning toward her. Unfortunately, because she was already so close, that move put their faces only a couple of inches apart. Breath met breath. "Is all of what you told me true?"

"Yes." She paused. Nodded. Paused again. "There are some blank spots in my memory, but giving birth isn't one of them. I swear I had a baby."

And he was the father.

Okay. He didn't doubt that last part. If Lexie had indeed had a child, then the timing was perfect for it to be his. Unfortunately, the pregnancy timing was the only thing that was perfect or that made sense.

She pressed her lips together for a moment and

gave him a considering stare. "I don't think I would have left your bed and gone to another man."

"You wouldn't have." In fact, in those days leading up to Billy Avery's trial, while Lexie had still been in his protective custody, they'd talked about a lot of things, including their sex lives.

Or lack thereof.

Lexie wasn't a person who slept around. Neither was he, despite the player reputation he had among his fellow officers.

Even though he tried to tamp down all the wild scenarios that started to fly through his head, he wasn't completely successful. But Garrett forced himself to focus.

First things first.

He ejected the ammunition from her weapon. The unfired bullets landed on the floor. Using his bare foot, he kicked them several feet away from her.

She watched the cartridges scatter, and her gaze flew to his again. "You still think I'm here to shoot you?"

"I don't want you to have the opportunity to even consider it. Confiscating and disarming a weapon are standard police procedures."

"If I were a suspect."

He shook his head. "I don't know *what* you are. Or what's going on. You broke into the home of a cop, which only makes things worse for you. And for me. I just want to follow some kind of rules and regs so I know I'll be doing something right."

Which was a joke that would have earned him some serious ribbing from his brother, sister and parents—all four of whom were cops or former cops. He'd never really thought of himself as a rule follower. However, in this case, he hoped the rules would ground him, because he needed something to do that.

"Who stole the baby?" he asked.

Just like that, the fight in her expression and posture faded. No more hiked up chin. No more adamant if-I-were-a-suspect retorts. "I don't know. As I said, I have gaps in my memory, and unfortunately that's one of them."

"All right." Those gaps wouldn't make this easier, but it wasn't impossible. "Start with what you do know."

She waited a moment, apparently considering his suggestion. "I know who I am. More or less. I remember my childhood, growing up on a ranch in east Texas with my father. I remember the day I left to go to college. It's my adulthood that's a little fuzzy. I can't recall working as a bodyguard for William Avery, and I didn't have any idea about his arrest or the trial."

Those weren't just gaps in her memory. They were huge craters that encompassed months of time. "And you didn't remember me?"

She drew in her breath, released it slowly. "No."

Garrett worked his way through the implications of what she was saying. For all practical purposes, *he* was a gap. "Then why did you come here to my house? How did you guess that we'd even had sex?"

"In one of the articles there was a photo of us leaving the courthouse. You had your arm curved around my waist and were obviously trying to get me out of the path of the photographers and the press."

He remembered the picture. In fact, he'd stared at it for hours after Lexie had left. "From that, you decided I'd fathered your baby?"

"There was something about the way you were holding me." She shrugged. "It was…intimate."

She looked at him.

He looked at her.

And it was still intimate.

Even now.

Hell. He could feel the attraction. Evidently that was something even gaps in memory couldn't cool down. Well, he sure as heck would put an end to it. He was not going to lose his badge by giving in to emotions that he should have never felt in the first place.

"Yeah. Intimate," he repeated. His boss had thought the same thing—so much so that the single photo had spurred some hard questions from Internal Affairs. Questions about Garrett's professionalism. About his dedication to the badge and his assignment.

Questions that had cut to the core simply because they'd been asked.

No.

He wasn't going back there.

"After you testified that day, you were upset. Rightfully so," Garrett explained, trying to make it sound clinical. "Billy Avery's lawyers had asked some tough questions and tried to rattle you while you were on the stand. They also tried to discredit you and your testimony about the illegal activity that you'd witnessed. But you held your ground. You were able to give details that the defense couldn't refute."

"And it was after I left the courthouse that we went to the hotel and…had sex?"

Garrett waited a moment. "You remember anything about that?"

"No."

That didn't matter. Because he had enough memories for both of them.

"And I don't remember leaving," she continued. "Though there was an article that mentioned I'd disappeared."

There was no way he could keep this clinical, so he settled for keeping it short. "You did."

She stared at him. "I don't know where I went. Where I stayed. What I did. All of that is a blank, and I don't remember anything until I went into labor."

Well, at least they had that. "You have no idea who took the child?"

"None. But I remember where it happened. It was at the Brighton Birthing Center."

The facility instantly rang a bell. There'd been some kind of altercation there recently, but he couldn't remember the details. "That's one of those back to nature places just outside the city limits?"

She nodded. "This isn't a real memory, but more like a vague recollection coupled with a theory. I went there when the labor started. Why, I don't know. Maybe because I was staying close by, or maybe because I knew someone who worked there. I delivered the baby. And then the doctor gave me that syringe filled with drugs. I think he did that so the other man could take the baby from me."

Despite her sketchy details, Garrett could almost see it. A sterile, milk-white delivery room. Lexie, weak from giving birth. At that moment, she was about as vulnerable as she could get.

"What happened next?" he asked.

"The doctor left me there in the birthing room. I managed to get off the bed, somehow. I went to look for the baby. But I was dizzy, and I couldn't see where the man had taken her. Then I heard the doctor telling the security guard to find me and make sure I didn't get out of there."

Garrett forced the emotion aside and dealt with the facts. "But you obviously escaped."

"Through the fire exit. I was still wearing a hospital gown, and I was barefoot. Not to mention I was drugged. I saw the man who took the baby. He put her in a dark blue van and sped away. I knew I wouldn't be able to stay conscious for long so I, uh, borrowed a car from the parking lot and tried to go after him."

Garrett ignored the *borrowed* part. He would deal with the stolen car issue if and when it came up again. "You weren't successful."

She shook her head. "No. I only made it a few miles, and I barely managed to get off the road and onto a path deep in the woods before I blacked out. When I came to, it was nearly two days later, and the man, the dark blue van and the baby were nowhere around."

He could almost see that, too. As a cop. And as a prospective parent. Neither viewpoint pleased him.

Mercy, did he really have a child out there somewhere?

A child who'd been born, and stolen, under the circumstances Lexie had just described? He certainly couldn't dismiss it, but he couldn't dismiss the problems in her account, either.

"When you regained consciousness, you didn't go to the police?" he asked.

"I tried." She made a soft, throaty sound of disapproval. Probably because it was obvious he was now interrogating her. "I was on my way there when someone ran me off the road. It was a cop."

Garrett felt his stomach tighten. "A cop?"

"Well, he was wearing a cop's uniform, anyway. I managed to get away. I drove the car back into the woods so the *cop* or anyone else on the road wouldn't be able to see me, but I was so weak that I passed out at the wheel again. Someone found me. A rancher. And he took me to a small county hospital and that's where I've been—in and out of consciousness, for nearly three weeks."

And with her having no wallet, ID or memory, the medical staff wouldn't have known whom to contact. Not that she had a next of kin—her parents were dead.

"Why didn't the doctors at the county hospital call the police?" Garrett asked.

"Because I begged them not to. I told them I was on the run from an abusive ex, that he'd beaten and drugged me. And I told them that my ex was a cop."

"And they bought all of that?"

She nodded. "They wanted to give me a gynecological exam. They thought maybe I'd been raped, but I assured them that a rape hadn't occurred, that I was simply having a heavier than usual menstrual cycle. I didn't want them discovering that I'd recently given birth, because it would have spurred too many questions, and it might have caused them to call the cops, after all. I couldn't risk that. I couldn't even stand on my own two feet, and I knew I wouldn't be able to fight off another attack."

Garrett considered everything she'd said. "Yet you weren't so weak that you couldn't come up with a whole list of apparently believable lies."

Oh, that earned him a glare. "Be thankful that the lies came easily. If they hadn't, I probably would be dead by now. And where would that have left the baby, huh?"

He wasn't ready to think about that just yet. But

soon. Very soon. "After you were discharged from the hospital—"

"I wasn't discharged," she interrupted. "Once I regained consciousness and some strength, I sneaked out. Because I was afraid someone would try to kill me again."

Her fear certainly seemed genuine, but like her memory, there were some huge gaps in her story. "And you still didn't go to the police?" he pressed.

"I didn't think I could trust the cops. Especially since it may have been a cop who ran me off the road." She turned away from him, in the direction of his dresser. She didn't exactly glance at his Glock, but Garrett figured she was well aware that it was there.

"Remember that part about not doing anything to rile me?" he warned.

"Well, you're riling me," she retorted. But she wasn't just kidding around. Anger chilled her voice, and she got right in his face. "Don't you get it? We have a baby out there, and someone has her. Do you think it's a good idea to stand around here wasting time with all these questions? We could be using this time to find her."

"Information and facts will help find her, and you seem to be seriously short on both."

"Because I can't remember!" she shouted. The burst of emotion left as quickly as it came. Her shoulders slumped. "*Please,* just believe me."

It was the please that got him. That, and the teary look. "And what if I do?"

A glimmer of hope flashed in her eyes. "I need to get back into the Brighton Birthing Center." She glanced at her gun, which he still held in his hand. "I wasn't sure I could even shoot straight. And I didn't know about the martial arts training. I figured if I went barging in there asking questions, I'd just get myself killed. After what happened with the cop trying to run me off the road, I figured I couldn't go to the police. Present company excluded, of course. I decided that since you were likely the baby's father, I should tell you."

So, there it was. In a nutshell. Even if he had doubts about the validity of her memory, he couldn't doubt that sincere *please*. But it didn't mean he'd agree to go off on some renegade chase. This had to be done by the book. He had to get his lieutenant involved.

Garrett opened his mouth to tell her, but that was as far as he got. He saw the movement out of the corner of his eye, behind her. To the right of the double French doors that led to his backyard.

"Get down," Garrett said. Not a shout; he practically whispered it. But it still came through loud and clear as an order.

Lexie tried to follow his gaze, no doubt to see what had triggered his reaction, but he didn't give her the chance. Garrett slapped off the light switch, plunging them into darkness. In the same motion, he hooked his arm around her waist and shoved her to the floor.

It was barely in time.

Because a bullet slammed through the one of the French doors, pelting them with a deadly spray of splintered wood and broken glass.

Chapter Four

It took a moment for Lexie to figure out what was happening. One second the French door was there. A second later, there was a gaping hole in it, and Garrett and she were being pelted with glass.

"He used a silencer," she heard Garrett say. Somehow. With her pulse pounding she was surprised she'd managed to hear anything.

But she fully understood that someone had just tried to murder them.

Lexie's heart kicked into overdrive. She hadn't thought her life could get any more complicated, but she'd obviously thought wrong.

"There are three of them out there," Garrett announced. "Maybe more."

Oh, God. It just kept getting worse. "All armed?"

"I only got a glimpse, but it appears that way."

The adrenaline and the fear slammed through her. Lexie wasn't helpless, but she certainly wasn't mentally or physically prepared to take on gunmen who would brazenly fire shots into a cop's house.

"I guess this isn't a good time for me to say I told you so," she mumbled. "You didn't believe me when I said someone was after me."

"Can we put this argument on hold, huh?" he snarled. "We've got a situation here."

Yes, a situation they might not survive.

Garrett scrambled across the room, and even though he'd turned out the lights, there was enough illumination from the moonlight filtering through the French doors that she could see him reach for his gun. In another smooth move he slid her weapon across the floor to her. Lexie took the cue and tried to retrieve the ammunition that he'd expelled minutes earlier. There was just one problem: she couldn't find it.

"I-told-you-so's aside, who's out there?" Garrett asked. He hurriedly locked the bedroom door. The simple gesture was a sickening reminder that the gunmen might not stay outside. They'd likely come in after them. "What are we up against?"

She waited a moment, praying the answer would come to her. It didn't. "I don't know."

And she didn't. Unfortunately, there were a lot of things she wasn't sure of, but she was certain of one thing—this attack was meant for her. Maybe it was the doctor. Or the man who'd actually stolen her baby. Maybe it was both. At this point it didn't matter. The only thing that mattered was staying alive so they could find their daughter.

"Call for backup," Garrett ordered, crawling across the room to the window. Using his bare foot, he kicked the ammunition and sent it rolling her way. "The phone's next to the bed. Stay low."

Lexie scooped up the bullets and reloaded as she scurried to the phone. She yanked it from its cradle, her index finger already poised to dial 911, but there was no dial tone.

"It's not working," she relayed to Garrett. "I think they cut the line."

He cursed. "You don't happen to have a cell phone on you?"

"No."

He mumbled something she couldn't distinguish. "Mine is in the kitchen."

"Enough said," she mumbled back. Because she knew the kitchen had lots and lots of windows, plus a glass patio door. Going in there would be suicide. Besides, it was probably the area the gunmen would no doubt choose to break and enter. It'd certainly been her first choice to gain access to the place.

Garrett lifted his head for a quick look out the French doors. It was necessary, she knew. He needed to assess the situation.

But she also knew he'd just risked being shot.

He'd put his life on the line, not necessarily for her, though. He was, after all, a cop through and through. And Lexie was counting heavily on that. Because she needed all his cop skills, all his re-solve—*everything*—to get out of this and find the baby.

"Are they still out there?" she asked, and was almost afraid to hear the answer.

"I don't see them." He paused. "That doesn't mean they aren't there."

Lexie silently agreed. She seriously doubted the gunmen would just leave. Which meant that Garrett and she needed a plan. There was just one problem. Three gunmen, maybe more, and she couldn't even remember if she knew how to shoot straight.

"I know how to use this gun, right?" she whispered.

"You know how." He glanced at her and made eye contact from across the room. "That doesn't mean you're going to get the opportunity to prove it."

"You have a better idea?"

"A better idea than shooting our way out of here? Yeah, I think I do. Follow me."

Crawling across the glass-littered floor, he went to the door that led into the hall, and pressed his ear against it.

She made her way toward him. To his side. And listened as well. She heard the mechanical rhythm of the air conditioner, but nothing else.

Garrett reached for the doorknob.

Lexie reached for him, latching on to his wrist. "We're going out there?"

"We don't have a choice." His voice was strained

and had little sound. "We have no way to call for backup, and with those silencers we can't count on the neighbors hearing anything and calling the cops."

It all made sense. Unfortunately. They couldn't just stay put. There was nothing to stop the gunmen from crashing through those French doors.

"You're just going to have to trust me on this," Garrett said.

He didn't give her time to respond. He took her hand from his wrist and opened the door. Just a fraction. He glanced out into the hallway and must have approved of what he saw, or rather what he didn't see, because he whispered, "Let's go."

Crouching, Garrett opened the door wide and had another quick look before he started out of the room. He moved in bursts, his vigilant gaze darting around the hall.

Lexie followed. Staying low. And keeping a firm grip on her gun.

They went toward the kitchen—the last place on earth she'd thought he would go. And that put a substantial dent in her resolve to trust him. Still, she continued to follow him, and she continued to pray. They had to make it out of this. Failure was not an option.

Lexie forced herself to remember her baby's cry. It was the only thing she could remember about the child she'd given birth to. But that cry was enough to sustain her, and Lexie held on to it as they inched their way across the kitchen floor.

The room was dark. Not by accident. She'd turned out the lights before she'd gone into the hall to confront Garrett. Maybe, just maybe, the darkness would shield them so they could go wherever Garrett was taking them.

She heard a sound. Not the baby's cry that she'd fixed in her head, but a snap. As if someone had stepped on a twig. The sound was close. Too close. It had likely come from the backyard, mere feet away.

Garrett paused. Lifted his head, listening. Another snap, closer this time. The doorknob on the kitchen door moved. Someone was testing to see if it was locked. Thankfully, it was. But that testing caused Garrett to look over his shoulder at her.

Even with just the dim moonlight, she saw his expression. Saw the question on his face. "I locked the patio door when I came in," she whispered. "I was afraid someone might follow me. Obviously, I was right to be afraid."

Not that a locked glass door would provide them with much protection.

Garrett evidently knew that as well, because he didn't look for his phone. He went straight to the laundry room, which was little more than a corridor. He didn't stop there. He reached up and grabbed keys from a wooden rack mounted on the wall, and unlocked the door that led into the garage.

There was a crash of glass from the kitchen. The gunmen were either inside or would be within seconds. Lexie felt another slam of adrenaline, and it gave her the jolt of energy that she needed.

Garrett opened the door and caught her arm, practically dragging her into the garage. He didn't waste a moment. He yanked open the driver's door of his vintage black Mustang and shoved her inside. Lexie scrambled into the passenger's seat so that Garrett could get behind the wheel and start the engine.

"Hang on and stay down," he warned.

And with that, he gripped the steering wheel with his left hand and gunned the motor. The car bolted forward, crashing through the garage door.

GARRETT HAD HOPED that his garage door wouldn't put up much resistance, but unfortunately, it did. A slab of it landed right in the middle of his windshield. The safety glass cracked, webbed and otherwise obstructed his view, but it stayed firmly in place.

He didn't dare put down his window and stick his head out so he could navigate, either. Not with three gunmen in the area. But he did turn on his headlights and floored the accelerator. He braced himself for the gunmen to shoot at them, braced himself for an all-out attack, and tried to keep his own gun steady.

"I don't think they're following us," he heard Lexie say.

He glanced at her and saw something that caused his blood pressure to spike.

She was looking out the back window.

Garrett immediately shoved her back down in the seat. "What part of *stay down* didn't you understand?"

"I might have to return fire. You concentrate on getting us out of here. I'll do what I need to do."

He couldn't argue with that. It was reasonable. Well, semi-reasonable. There wasn't a lot about this situation that qualified as *reasonable*. Still, he truly might need her to return fire if this evolved into a gun battle. He didn't like the three-to-one odds if he had to do this alone. But then, he didn't care much relying for backup on someone with memory issues.

Garrett checked the side mirror and was a little surprised at what he saw. He was also slightly relieved. An empty street stretched out behind them. So maybe the gunmen hadn't pursued them. For now, anyway.

But he couldn't count on them just giving up.

"Go back through the bits of memory you have," Garrett insisted. "And come up with a theory as to who just tried to kill us."

"The doctor with me during the delivery," she readily answered. "The man who took the baby. Or the cop who ran me off the road."

Three suspects. Three gunmen. Coincidence? "And you don't know who any of these men are?"

She shook her head. "No. But I intend to find out."

"Because they're the only ones who might know where the baby is."

He hadn't meant to say that aloud. Heck, he hadn't even meant to think it. He couldn't devote a lot of mental energy to the baby now. Mainly because he didn't know if there was a child. And if their daughter had actually been born, he needed to get Lexie to safety before he started to unravel this deadly puzzle she'd brought to him. Even if there wasn't a child, it was abundantly clear that someone was after Lexie.

And him.

The shot that'd come through his bedroom could have been aimed at either of them. Or both. And if they hadn't immediately turned out the lights and gotten down on the floor, Garrett had no doubts that there would have been a second shot. Probably a third. There would have been as many bullets as it took to eliminate them.

This had not been a warning. It'd been a cold, calculated attempt to execute them.

Why?

He checked the mirror again, and when he saw that things were still clear, he slowed to a reasonable speed and took the turn to the highway.

"Where are we going?" Lexie asked.

He didn't answer her, because he knew it was an answer she wouldn't like. Even with the possibility that a cop was involved in this, he had no choice. He was going to police headquarters.

Garrett only hoped it wasn't a fatal mistake.

Chapter Five

Garrett took a huge gulp of the god-awful coffee that the rookie officer had given him, then he signed the statement he'd just prepared about the shooting "incident." He hoped the caffeine would help with the headache that throbbed in both temples. Spent adrenaline was a witch to deal with, and he didn't have the time to let the effects wear off naturally.

He needed a clear head, and he needed it now.

Across the room, seated on the break room sofa, Lexie was finishing up her handwritten statement and sipping coffee as well. She was also making the same disapproving expression at the bitter taste. Well, that was partly the reason for her expression.

Some of it was aimed at him.

All right. Most of it was aimed at him.

"I hope I don't have to say I told you so again," Lexie grumbled. Practically tearing through the sheets of paper with the tip of the pen, she signed her name to the report and tossed it onto the table.

It wasn't the first time she'd voiced that complaint since they'd arrived at police headquarters an hour earlier. Garrett didn't think it would be the last, either.

Nope.

He was in for a night of her complaints. Garrett just hoped those objections weren't warranted. Because it might be awhile before he could figure out if coming here had indeed been a bad idea. It might be longer still before he could discover if there was a departmental leak. Or worse, a would-be departmental killer who had a penchant for running women off the road.

Garrett dropped his statement on top of Lexie's and checked the clock mounted on the wall. His brother, Lieutenant Brayden O'Malley, would be arriving within minutes. The shooting and those gunmen put this case right in his brother's lap. However, even if it hadn't fallen within Brayden's realm of responsibility, Garrett had no plans to go to anyone else. He'd already decided to keep this investigation close to the vest.

Or rather, in the family.

"We're wasting time," Lexie continued. She practically slapped the foam cup of coffee on the adjacent table, and got up to pace.

"We're staying alive," Garrett corrected. "That is what you want, right?"

Lexie stopped pacing only long enough to send a narrowed, fiery glance his way. "I thought you believed me about the baby."

Her words sent a jab of pain through his right

temple. He'd meant to set this whole issue aside until they'd resolved the gunmen situation, but he now knew he couldn't. "I believe you believe it."

She stopped again. Right in front of him. Mere inches away. "Refresh my memory—are you always this pigheaded?"

"Always."

Lexie huffed and squared her shoulders. She was probably aiming for a show of strength, but failed miserably. Because there was nothing she could do to dissolve that look in her eyes. The pain.

The fear.

He wasn't unaffected by that look, either. Despite all the bad blood between them, there were other things between them as well. The past that stained their present relationship was one he couldn't forget.

With her broken memories, Lexie was lucky. In that respect. She probably didn't remember the attraction that had started all of this. It was too bad he couldn't give himself a little dose of selective amnesia. It would help him focus on getting those men who'd tried to kill them.

"I remember something," she said out of the blue.

Garrett pulled himself away from the unwanted trip down memory lane so he could make eye contact. She was staring at him. No. She was *studying* him.

"You remembered who's trying to kill you?" he asked.

She blinked. Shook her head. And it seemed as if

she'd changed her mind about what she'd been on the verge of saying. "No. Not that. It's not important."

He grabbed her arm when she tried to step away. "Excuse me? Your memory returning isn't important?" And he made sure his voice was dripping with cynicism.

"It's not my full memory. It's *a* memory. As in one. One memory that I shouldn't have even mentioned."

"Why?" he asked before he thought it through. And he was immediately sorry about that. Because he saw the blush spread across her cheeks. "Oh," he mumbled. "You remembered us having sex."

"Not quite. But I, uh, remembered the kiss leading up to it."

That was some memory to regain. Garrett remembered that kiss, as well. Unfortunately, he remembered it in full, blazing detail. And probably because he was standing so close to Lexie, the memory was as crystal clear as the original.

"It's still there," Lexie said, looking up at him. "The attraction," she explained.

As if he needed any clarification.

"It's there," he admitted, since a lie that big would have stuck in his throat. "But bad things happened the last time we acted on that attraction."

She flinched. "You mean the baby."

"No." His quick response surprised him almost as much as it obviously surprised her. "*If* there is a baby, then that's not a bad thing."

He meant it. He'd never considered himself father material, but if there was a child, then he would love his baby and do whatever it took to get her back and keep her safe.

"Thank you," Lexie whispered.

The emotion in her voice drew his gaze back to hers. "For what?"

"For caring about the baby."

Oh, man. There were tears in her eyes. Tears! Again. He couldn't keep resisting her. He would have almost certainly pulled her into his arms to offer what meager comfort he could offer.

But he didn't get a chance.

"Want to tell me what's going on here?" he heard someone ask.

But not just anyone. His brother, Brayden.

Garrett shifted his attention to the doorway and spotted his older sibling standing there. Even though Brayden had been called in well after normal duty hours, he still managed to look very much like a cop in charge. He was wearing khakis and a crisp white shirt. Tucked in, of course. He had his badge clipped to his belt.

Garrett suddenly felt very unprofessional in the black T-shirt and boots he'd grabbed from his locker. Still, the too casual attire was far better than the alternative. When he'd arrived at headquarters, he'd only been wearing jeans.

"Well? What's going on here?" Brayden repeated.

He glanced at Lexie, and though his expression changed only slightly, Garrett saw the disapproval in his brother's eyes.

"It's not what you think," Garrett insisted.

And he knew his brother well enough to know that what Brayden was thinking wasn't good. Brayden no doubt believed that Lexie was back in Garrett's life. Not back in an ordinary sense, either.

But in a sexual sense.

His eyes met Brayden's and a dozen questions passed between them. Before Garrett answered those questions, he motioned for his brother to come inside the break room, and Garrett shut the door.

"Lexie," Brayden said in greeting, walking toward her. He reached down and picked up the statements from the table.

She shook her head, glanced at Garrett.

"She doesn't remember you," Garrett explained. "Someone gave her a drug, and it's caused some memory loss."

Brayden stayed quiet a moment, but Garrett knew he was processing the information. "And that's why you're here?"

"We're here because Garrett thought he could trust you," Lexie interjected. "Can he?"

"With his life," Brayden readily answered. "But I'd still like an explanation about what's going on."

The three exchanged glances. Garrett decided to go first. "Someone fired a shot into my house tonight.

There were three of them. All armed. I had to drive out of there fast."

Brayden took a deep breath. "Were either of you hurt?"

"No," Garrett assured him. "But we have a problem. I can't ID any of the gunmen, and I have a feeling they aren't going to stop with just this one attempt."

"So, why haven't you made this investigation official? Why call me in and close the door?"

Lexie stepped between them. "Because I have reason to believe that it might be a cop who wants me dead."

His brother was very good at hiding his emotions but he wasn't able to hide his shock, and perhaps his disbelief. "I'll want an explanation about that, too."

Before that could happen, there was a knock at the door, one sharp rap, and it opened. The rookie stuck his head inside. "Lieutenant O'Malley?" he said to Brayden. "Lieutenant Dillard is on the phone. He wants to speak to you."

"Hell," Garrett grumbled. Lieutenant Dillard was his boss, and since he wanted to speak to Brayden, that probably meant the conversation would be about Lexie and him.

"Did you happen to tell Lieutenant Dillard I was here?" Garrett asked the rookie.

"I did. Because he asked," the young officer quickly added. "Your neighbor saw some suspicious men hanging around your house, and he reported it. The neighbor said someone bashed into your garage door."

Great. This just kept getting messier and messier.

"I'll be right back," Brayden said, heading for the door.

"Wait," Lexie called out. Brayden stopped and turned back around to face her. He met her gaze head-on. "Remember what I told you."

She no doubt meant the part about the possible cop who'd tried to kill her.

"You'll just have to trust me to do my job," Brayden responded. With that, he turned and walked out.

"Trust," Lexie mumbled. "It's disconcerting how easily that word flows right off the tongue. Let's hope it's a word that actually means something."

Garrett shook his head. "My brother won't do anything to hurt us."

"Maybe not intentionally."

Since that was the truth, Garrett decided it was a good time to finish his coffee. Unfortunately, it was cold and had seemingly turned to gasoline. But because his head was still pounding, he forced himself to drink it.

Lexie sank onto the sofa with a heavy sigh and leaned her head against the cushion. "Why does your brother hate me?"

Garrett hadn't been prepared for her question. "Who said he hates you?"

"I did. I could tell by the way he looked at me."

And here he thought his brother had the ultimate poker face. "It has to do with what happened when your boss, Billy Avery, was on trial."

"Oh. He thinks I helped Billy commit those crimes." But then she hesitated. "No. What your brother feels for me is personal, isn't it?"

Because of the headache, the fatigue, and because this was a subject he didn't really want to discuss, Garrett nearly pulled a silent act. But this was bound to come up sometime or another, and he wanted her to hear it from him. Or rather, he wanted her to hear the sanitized version.

"Brayden doesn't like you because when you unofficially left my protective custody, you officially put me in a really bad place with my boss and just about everyone in the D.A.'s office."

She lifted her head, studied him. "I see."

"The D.A. was lucky to get a conviction without the rest of your testimony." And Garrett hadn't wanted to think just how bad things could have gotten for him if Avery hadn't been convicted. If he'd walked, the D.A. would have looked for someone to hang, and Garrett would have been the one they'd come after.

With reason.

He'd failed to do his job, by allowing a material witness to escape custody. Of course, he'd also failed to do his job by having sex with that witness. In this case, two wrongs definitely didn't make a right.

"Your brother knows what happened between us?" Lexie asked.

"He knows."

She stared at him. "And you still think he'll be willing to help me?"

"I know he will." But what Garrett didn't know was the form that help might take. Brayden wasn't the sort of cop to keep things under the table, but Garrett was hoping his brother would do it this time.

The door opened and Brayden came back in.

"Well?" Garrett immediately asked.

He frowned. "I chose my words carefully."

Garrett didn't know whose sigh of relief was bigger—his or Lexie's. But there was no hint of relief in Brayden's expression.

"Lieutenant Dillard knows that Lexie has some issues to be worked out. Personal issues that he's agreed to let me handle at my discretion."

That brought Lexie off the sofa. *"You?"*

"Me," Brayden enunciated. "Because Lieutenant Dillard insisted that Garrett not have any official contact with you." He held up his hand, cutting off the protest that Garrett was about to make. "Dillard is right. You can't be involved in this, Garrett. Because if this—whatever *this* is—ends up going to the D.A., then it could cost you your badge. The D.A. hasn't forgotten what happened the last time you were involved with Lexie."

"Your badge?" Lexie questioned.

Garrett certainly couldn't deny what his brother was saying.

"Do Mom and Dad know she's back?" Brayden asked.

Lexie huffed. "What, I riled your parents, too?"

Brayden shrugged. "If you rile one O'Malley, you rile us all."

Her gaze flew from Brayden's to his. "Well, I'm sorry. I truly am. But I wouldn't have come back into Garrett's life if it hadn't been for the baby."

Dead silence fell over the room.

"Baby?" Brayden repeated.

Oh, man.

Garrett so wished he'd had a chance to explain this first. But one thing was for sure—he'd get a chance to explain the baby *now*.

Chapter Six

"I had a baby, a daughter," Lexie said. She cleared her throat. "Garrett's child."

She stared at the lieutenant and waited for his reaction. There was no mistaking that this was Garrett's brother. Brayden was slightly older, probably mid-thirties, and there was a serenity and calmness about him that Garrett seriously lacked. But the older O'Malley had the same dark brown hair, the same classically handsome face and the same green eyes.

Seeing those facial features made her think of her daughter. She didn't even know the color of her baby's eyes.

"Your baby?" Brayden questioned his brother.

Garrett nodded.

She had to hand it to the lieutenant. She'd just delivered what had to be shocking news, but other than that one question and a slightly lifted right eyebrow that he aimed at Garrett, that was it. The calmness and serenity remained fully intact.

"Things are complicated," Garrett explained.

That raised eyebrow lowered. "Even complicated things can be explained."

Yes, but not without lots and lots of emotion. Each time Lexie had to retell the story, each time she had to think about it, it was as if someone were ripping open her soul. She'd lost her child, and nothing could heal that wound until her daughter was found.

"Someone stole the baby right after Lexie gave birth," Garrett continued. He set his coffee aside. "She didn't go to the police because someone tried to kill her, and she thought that person was a cop."

"I see," Brayden said. "Well, that sort of negates this whole issue of you not being involved in the investigation, doesn't it? If this concerns your baby—"

"There's more. We really need to talk." Garrett took his brother by the arm and started for the door.

"Where are you going?" Lexie immediately asked.

"Brayden and I need to have a private conversation."

She put her hands on her hips and stared at them. "Why? So you can tell him that the baby might be a figment of my drug-induced imagination? Well, she isn't, and I thought those gunmen proved that."

Garrett shook his head. "The only thing they proved was that they were gunmen. They could have been sent by Billy Avery. He might want you eliminated so you can't testify against him if he's ever granted an appeal."

Lexie desperately wanted to dismiss the theory.

But she couldn't. Even though she didn't remember her former boss, from what she'd read about him on the Internet, he was capable of pretty much anything. Still, that didn't discount the fact that she knew she'd had a baby, and that baby was missing.

Brayden checked his watch. "It's nearly 10:00 p.m., but I think I can arrange to speak to Avery at the prison. I wouldn't mind asking him a few questions."

"Neither would I," Garrett agreed.

Brayden didn't offer to give him an opportunity. Nor did he waste any time. He headed out of the room, presumably to make that call.

Lexie didn't waste any time, either. "The baby is real," she insisted.

"And so is Billy Avery," Garrett countered.

Her first reaction was to throw her hands in the air and walk out, but that wasn't a smart idea. "I need you to *trust* me on this," she said, using his own words. "I need us to work together because we have to find her."

Unlike his brother, Garrett wasn't very good at hiding his emotions. There was a mixture of frustration and irritation in his eyes.

"My lieutenant ordered me to stay away from you." But it didn't seem as if Garrett was talking to her but to himself. Sort of a reminder. Or maybe it was the bottom line of a private argument he was having.

She didn't blame him. His boss had ordered hands off. She was essentially Garrett's own personal leper.

And besides, she didn't doubt that Brayden O'Malley was a competent cop. He could probably do what was necessary.

Probably.

But even though that *probably* verified the doubts she was having about this situation, she was certain that she couldn't ask Garrett to risk his badge. After all, she was the one who'd set up this scenario of putting his career in jeopardy in the first place. She couldn't ask him to go through that again.

"Your brother will help me look for the baby," she said, and she tried not to make it sound like a question.

Garrett nodded. "He'll do everything humanly possible."

That and the accompanying nod did seem like questions.

Confusing questions.

Moments later, Garrett cursed. "I can't walk away from this."

It took a moment for her to get past the profanity and grasp what he'd said. It took another moment for her to gather her breath. "What do you mean?"

He crammed his hands into his jeans pocket and shifted uneasily. "If someone took my child, I can't stand back and let my brother do what I should be doing."

Oh, she grasped that all right. And she grasped the implications of it. "But your badge—"

"If our baby exists, I will find her."

Lexie hated what this might cost him, but relief flooded through her. Yes, Brayden was more than an adequate substitute, but he was still a substitute. She figured a father would be more likely to put his life on the line for his own child. And unfortunately, she was afraid their lives would have to be on the line. Hadn't the earlier incident already proved that was true? That, coupled with a massive amount of luck, might help them find the baby.

"I'll request some vacation time," he continued. "We'll be discreet. We won't tell anyone other than Brayden what we're doing, and we'll investigate what's happened."

There it was. The assurance she'd prayed for since she first saw that picture of them and realized he was the father of her child.

"Thank you," she whispered. She tried to blink back the tears, but one escaped.

He reached out and wiped it away with his thumb.

It was a big mistake, being that close to him, especially with the emotions, and the hope, racing out of control. Even with the graveness of their situation, she still felt that slam of attraction. She still felt that hungry, desperate kiss that they'd shared months ago.

How ironic that she couldn't remember critical details of her life, but she could recall every nuance of that kiss.

His taste.

The feel of his mouth against hers.

The raw heat.

She didn't need other memories to know that it was the most memorable kiss she'd ever had.

"We can't get involved again," he told her.

Okay. So, he was perhaps remembering that kiss, as well. He was also right. If they found their daughter, his lieutenant might not reprimand him too hard for his renegade investigation. But another personal involvement with Lexie, the leper?

No. The lieutenant wouldn't just let that go.

Staring into her eyes, Garrett slid his fingers beneath her chin. Lifted it slightly. And he inched toward her. Lexie felt paralyzed. She couldn't move. Couldn't think.

But she could feel.

Mercy, could she feel.

He stopped, his mouth only an inch or so from hers. She stopped, too. And they really looked at each other. In the depths of all that green, she went past the lust and saw all the doubts.

Reasonable doubts.

Sane, logical doubts.

"We'll concentrate on finding the baby and the person who's responsible," Garrett insisted.

Lexie nodded and stepped back. Unfortunately, she didn't do so quickly enough. The door opened and Brayden walked in. His cop's eyes didn't miss how close to each other Garrett and she were standing.

"Am I interrupting anything?" he asked.

"No." Garrett and she answered in unison. Quickly. And they both took huge steps back.

His brother studied them in a scrutinizing way that normally only strict parents and elementary school teachers could manage. "I arranged a video call with Billy Avery." He hitched his thumb in the direction of the hall. "We can take it in my office."

She was pleased and a little surprised that he'd managed that so quickly. "What exactly are you planning to ask Avery?"

"Don't worry. The questions won't be about you or the baby. I certainly don't want to tip our hand. Whatever our hand is," Brayden added in a mumble. "That means I want both of you to stay out of camera range so Avery can't see you."

"You're sure about that?" Garrett stepped ahead of her to walk alongside his brother. "I could persuade him to talk."

That earned him a lifted eyebrow from the lieutenant. "I don't think intimidation is the way to approach this."

"Maybe it is," Lexie interjected, moving to Garrett's side. "If Avery's the one who tried to have us killed, maybe intimidation is the fastest way to get answers."

She got a lifted eyebrow, too. For such a simple facial gesture, it conveyed a lot of disapproval.

Brayden opened his office door and ushered them inside. There was a uniformed officer at the cluttered oak desk, and he turned the monitor in Brayden's direction and excused himself.

"Both of you move away from the camera," Brayden insisted.

Garrett and she did as they were told, but angled themselves in the corner so they could view the monitor. Lexie wanted to see her former boss's face. Not only might it help her with those memory gaps, but she wanted to watch how he reacted when the lieutenant questioned him.

Brayden verified their positions, then pressed a button on the monitor. A man's face immediately appeared on the screen. There was no mistaking that this was Billy Avery. He looked exactly as he did in the newspaper photos. It wasn't the face of a Brandolike godfather. No. He was only thirty-one, just two years older than she was. His flame-red hair was slicked back in a style that probably would have appeared stark on anyone but him. But even in a prison uniform, Avery still managed to look fashionable.

And cocky.

He grinned at Brayden. "Lieutenant O'Malley. Long time no see. What can I do for you?" There was no politeness in his voice, and the question seemed almost like a challenge.

"I wondered if you were up to your old tricks," Brayden countered.

"Me?" Avery chuckled. "Haven't you heard? I'm

a changed man. Straight and narrow path. Law-abiding citizen."

Brayden just stared at him. "I checked your visitors' log. Yesterday morning, you had a fifteen-minute chat with one of your former employees. A man named Ted Benson."

The name meant nothing to Lexie, but it obviously meant something to Avery. No chuckle or grin. His mouth tightened slightly. "And why would a visit from an old friend interest you, Lieutenant?"

"Everything you do interests me," Brayden answered. "But what interests me more is what Ted Benson did after he spoke with you."

"I don't know what you mean." But while the denial sounded cocky, there was nothing cocky about his expression. Billy Avery was a concerned and perhaps perplexed man.

"Of course you do." And with that, Brayden reached down and ended the call.

"Wait a minute!" Lexie practically ran toward him. "You didn't find out if he hired the gunmen."

"But he soon will," Garrett calmly explained.

Brayden nodded. "I've already assigned someone to question Ted Benson and put him under surveillance. If Avery ordered him to come after you, then we'll soon know. Plus the wardens will monitor Avery's calls and visits."

"They can do that?"

"Oh, yes. Unless it's a meeting between Avery

and his lawyer, but I don't think his lawyer had anything to do with this."

So everything was in motion. Maybe when the officer questioned Ted Benson, he'd confess to orchestrating all of this. Except...

"The baby was taken over three weeks ago," Lexie explained. "Did this Ted Benson guy visit Avery around that time?"

Brayden shook his head. "He didn't have any visits that entire week. That doesn't mean he couldn't have set everything up prior to then. He could have arranged for someone to watch you, and wait until you went into labor." He picked up a black-and-white photo and handed it to her. "That's Ted Benson. Does he look familiar?"

Lexie studied the photograph of the dark-haired man. "No."

"He wasn't the man who took the child from you?"

"I don't think so. But I can't actually remember the man."

"How about the doctor?" Brayden asked. "What do you remember about him?"

"Not much. Everything's sort of hazy. He had touches of gray in his hair. Wide shoulders. And, of course, I do remember the shot he gave me."

Brayden and Garrett made eye contact. "But you're positive you gave birth?"

She groaned. "Positive."

"How can you be so sure? Have you had a doctor verify it?"

"I don't need it verified. What I need is to find my daughter."

Garrett eased her out of Brayden's face. "I'm sorry," he said to his brother.

"Sorry for what?" Lexie didn't like the direction of this conversation.

"Sorry that I didn't do what I should have done." He caught Lexie's arm. "And now it's time to find out for sure if we're parents or not."

Chapter Seven

Garrett paced up and down the hospital corridor because pacing was about the only thing he could do. Waiting wasn't easy for him under normal circumstances, and waiting to hear if he was indeed a father was about as far from normal as normal could get.

A father.

Him!

Man, fate sure had a strange sense of humor. His brother, Brayden, was the father of three. Now that was someone who was father material. Calm. Easygoing. Stable. Brayden took plenty of risks in his job as head of Homicide, but he always put his family first. Ditto for his sister, Katelyn. Though she didn't have children yet, she was the perfect aunt and was looking forward to the day when she would become a mother.

And then there was Garrett.

He loved his nephews and his niece, but fatherhood had never been in his plan. Actually, he'd only had one plan from about the age of six. He wanted to the best cop in the state of Texas. Garrett figured to get there, he'd have to make sacrifices, and one of those sacrifices would be a total commitment to the badge.

But the next few minutes could change all of that.

Just behind the door to the hospital clinic, the doctor was examining Lexie. One way or another, the man would be able to tell them if her memories were real.

And if they were real, that meant there was a baby.

Of course, this was just the start. If Lexie's memories were wrong, then they still had to deal with those gunmen. If the memories were accurate, they had to deal with the whole scope of being parents, finding a stolen child and figuring out who'd tried to kill them.

Garrett rarely felt overwhelmed, but he was sure feeling it now.

The door opened, and Dr. Northrop motioned for him to come in. Garrett's stomach actually knotted. It knotted even more when he spotted Lexie sitting on the end of the examining table. She was pale. Too pale. And she was trembling.

"Are you okay?" he asked her.

She nodded, but Garrett knew that nod was a lie.

"You might want to sit down," the elderly doctor instructed, and he pointed to a rolling metal chair by Lexie. Dr. Northrop leaned back against the door. "I can't pinpoint an exact date for the delivery, but I estimate about three and a half weeks. That coincides with what Ms. Rayburn told me."

That knot in Garrett's stomach got significantly tighter. "Are you saying there's really a baby?"

The doctor shrugged, pulled off his thick glasses and perched them on his graying head. "I have no way of knowing if the child survived, but Ms. Rayburn definitely gave birth."

"She survived," Lexie whispered. "I heard her cry."

All right. Garrett was glad he was sitting down. He glanced at Lexie, but she dodged his gaze. Maybe because she was riled that he hadn't believed her in the first place. Or maybe because hearing a confirmation was a little more than she'd been prepared to handle. But then, there was that last part. The part about maybe the baby hadn't survived. Except Garrett had no intention of believing that. That theory just didn't feel right.

"Ms. Rayburn appears to have healed properly," Dr. Northrop continued, his voice a little ragged with fatigue. "But I want to do lab tests to check her iron levels and such. I also want to try to identify what she was given that could have caused the memory loss. I figure it was some kind of narcotic. Perhaps morphine. In large doses, it can induce varying levels of amnesia. Unfortunately, there's not a way to reverse it, but sometimes the lost memories return on their own without medical assistance."

Both Lexie and Garrett just nodded. The memory loss was a big issue, but at the moment it seemed trivial.

Lexie and he were parents.

"I'd like to admit Ms. Rayburn to the hospital tonight," the doctor continued.

"No," she stated. And she left no room for argument. Probably because she realized that in a hospital bed, she'd be an easy target for those gunmen. Plus a hospital stay wouldn't help find their child. Still, Lexie wasn't well, and the drug that the doctor had given her could have caused damage that might require medication.

"Can you help her if she's hospitalized?" Garrett asked.

"Perhaps." Dr. Northrop didn't sound certain. Heck, he didn't even sound optimistic. "As I said, I could do some tests."

"The tests can wait," Lexie insisted.

The doctor obviously didn't care for her decision, but he nodded as if he'd expected it. "Even though you're recovering on schedule," he added, "you should probably refrain from sexual intercourse for at least a few more days. By four weeks, your body should have had enough time to get back to normal."

Sex. Great. Yet something else that seemed trivial, and had Garrett never believed he'd think *that*. Besides, he almost welcomed the doctor's instructions. If by some insane chance Lexie and he were to think about acting on the attraction between them, the doctor's orders would stand in the way. At least temporarily.

Dr. Northrop waited a moment, probably to see if

they had anything to say. When they didn't, he murmured, "I'll just give you two a couple of minutes so you can talk things over."

He didn't wait for them to respond, but walked out, leaving them alone.

Garrett took a minute to figure out the best way to grovel, and decided there wasn't one. So he went for the direct approach. "I'm sorry I didn't believe you," he declared, because he didn't know what the hell else to say. A thousand things were going through his head, and he wasn't coming to terms with any of them.

"We have to find her," Lexie mumbled.

Yes, they did.

Because she looked ready to collapse, or cry, he reached out, but then stopped himself. For a few seconds, anyway. He finally thought to heck with it, got up and pulled her into his arms.

There was a low sound, deep within her throat. A sad, mournful sound that he totally understood. They had a daughter. But she was missing. Or worse.

Garrett refused to think about that *worse*.

"I'll talk to Billy Avery," he promised. "If he's behind this, I'll find out, and I'll get him to tell me where he has her."

"I'm not sure Avery had anything to with this." She pulled back slightly and faced him. "There have been no demands for my cooperation. If he had her taken as leverage so that I wouldn't testify against him if he's granted a new trial, then why hasn't he used her to try to blackmail me?"

Garrett could think of a reason. Maybe Avery was keeping the child as an insurance policy. If so, Avery wouldn't do or say anything to threaten Lexie unless it became necessary. That meant her former boss would keep the baby alive, but Garrett couldn't stomach the idea of what kind of inadequate child care arrangements a man like Billy Avery would make. To him, the baby would be just a pawn.

That required Garrett to take a deep breath.

It was a little more than he could manage to think of a helpless baby—*his baby*—at the mercy of a convicted felon.

"I think I should go to the Brighton Birthing Center," Lexie said. "I'm positive that's where I had her, and that's where she was stolen."

Garrett was already shaking his head before she finished. "The last time you were there, someone tried to kill you with a drug overdose."

Still, he knew she was right. A visit to the birthing center was a good idea. It just wasn't a good idea for Lexie to do the visiting.

"I'll go there," he insisted. "Right after I talk with Billy Avery and after I've arranged protective custody for you."

Lexie did some head shaking of her own. "I know the layout of the birthing center. I took a virtual tour on the Internet. And if I see the doctor, I'll recognize him. Plus just being there might jog some of these hidden memories."

"It might jog some of the doctor's memories, too," Garrett reminded her. "And he might decide to finish the job he started."

"If he's there, he won't recognize me if I go in disguise."

Garrett considered that. And dismissed it. "It's too dangerous."

"Doing nothing could be far more dangerous. We could go there together—discreetly. We could pretend we're there to ask questions about the facility itself. And we can possibly find our baby."

"We could get killed," he countered.

"True. But it's a chance we'll have to take, Garrett. You know it and I know it."

Yes. And that was the bottom line. Despite his brother's warnings about not getting involved with Lexie, he had to, and if Garrett told Brayden about that involvement, it would only delay what had to be done. Brayden would insist on following at least a few of the rules and regs. They had to do whatever it took to find their baby. That meant going to the last place on earth he wanted Lexie to go—the Brighton Birthing Center.

He checked his watch. It was already after midnight. That was well past normal visiting hours, so the visit would have to wait until morning. Besides, Lexie and he needed to come up with a disguise for her. And they needed to get some sleep so they'd have clear heads when they went into the lion's den.

Oh, man.

He immediately thought of a different kind of lion's den.

Sleep meant they needed a place to lie down. They couldn't stay at his house. Much too risky. He wanted to keep this danger away from the family, too. Going to his parents or siblings might bring the danger right to their doorsteps. After all, those gunmen were still out there.

So that left a safe house or a hotel. It would take hours, or longer, to arrange for the house. There was also an extremely high probability that Brayden would order Garrett not to stay with Lexie at either place. That couldn't happen. He needed to be with her so they could make plans for their visit to the clinic.

Well, that and they had to come to terms with the fact they were parents of a missing baby girl.

A hotel was their best bet. He could use an unmarked police car to get them there. He could take a circuitous route to make sure they weren't followed. He could pay cash so there'd be no credit card trail. In other words, he could make it as safe as possible. And, in the morning they could visit the Brighton Birthing Center.

He only hoped all his security measures would keep Lexie alive.

And even more, he hoped he could survive spending the night with her.

"Two rooms wouldn't have made sense," Garrett said as he used the key card to unlock the hotel room door.

"I agree," Lexie told him. And she did. After what they'd been through, safety was one of their major concerns.

Of course, the baby was at the top of the list.

Somewhere on that list, perhaps a lot higher than either of them wanted, was the fact that they were about to share a hotel room. Alone. Together.

In a king-size bed.

There'd been no rooms with double beds available, and neither of them had been in the mood to go searching for one. It'd taken an hour of driving around the city just to make sure they hadn't been followed. It'd taken nearly a dozen calls to find a hotel that would take a cash deposit rather than a credit card. Then, it'd taken a trip to the ATM so Garrett would have the cash required. By then, neither of them had made a peep of protest about a single room with only one bed.

Lexie reminded herself that they were both exhausted, and they had to get some sleep so they could wake up early and work out the details of their visit to the birthing center. Plus, there was the doctor's suggestion that she refrain from having sex. So there it was. All spelled out for her. Not that she was even considering sex. No, she'd need energy for that. And a cooperating partner.

She was willing to bet that Garrett didn't fall into that cooperating partner category. She certainly didn't. But there did seem to be this weird involuntary energy simmering between them. Lexie had no trouble understanding how that energy had led them to where they were now.

Parents.

"I'll make some calls in the morning," Garrett explained once they were inside. "I'll get something we can use to disguise you. We'll work out what we're going to say. After we're back from the center, I'll figure out how I can legally get into the prison to have a chat with Billy Avery."

He locked the door behind them, engaged the security hasp and then promptly moved a huge chair in front of the door to block it.

"This is just a precaution," he added when he glanced at her.

Only then did Lexie realize that she probably looked scared. There was a good reason for that. She *was* scared. Not so much for her safety, but if something happened to Garrett and her that could leave their child in a horrible position.

"My advice is when we get to the center," Garrett continued, "you let me do most of the talking."

She started with a huff, but it quickly became a

sigh of frustration. "I'm not an idiot, Garrett. I wouldn't say anything—"

"Saying anything at all could be dangerous. Someone there might not recognize you in disguise, but they might recognize your voice."

"Oh." She hadn't even considered that. Not good. Because it immediately made her wonder about all the other things she might not have considered. Still, it didn't matter. Going into this with broken memories and an exhausted body wasn't ideal, but it wouldn't stop her. Nothing would stop her.

"I won't ask questions unless it's necessary," she assured him. She sat down on the foot of the bed, and her muscles practically cheered at the reprieve. "While you're doing all the talking, I'll just watch for a familiar face."

Garrett stood looking down at her. "And if you see a familiar face, you won't tackle the person and try to karate kick the truth out of him or her?"

For some strange reason that made her smile. Not a smile of amusement, but it was gratifying to think of her pulverizing the person responsible for all of this.

Lexie's smile faded when her thoughts returned to her daughter. "I just want to find out where that man took her, and someone at the clinic should be able to tell us that."

"Yes," Garrett said. A moment later, he repeated it. He sank down onto the opposite side of the bed— as far away from her as he could possibly get and still remain on the mattress. "I've been thinking about that—where they might have taken her."

So had Lexie. "If Billy Avery's behind this, then she could be anywhere." And that broke her heart.

"But if Avery's people have her, she's safe. Avery would want to keep her safe and sound so he could use her for leverage."

"Safe. But not necessarily all right." More thoughts came. Ones that Lexie had been trying to stave off, but this time, she wasn't successful. "She could be hungry. I don't know if they would bother to feed her when she needs a bottle. Or if they'd change her diaper—"

"You can't do this, Lexie. It'll tear you apart."

She turned her head and looked at him. One glance and she realized he knew what he was talking about. She could see the pain and the fear in his own eyes. Garrett, too, had all these shared concerns about their baby.

And neither of them could do a thing about it.

"Get some rest," he insisted. "You'll need it for tomorrow."

Lexie was too weary to argue, even though they had so many details to work out. She crawled to the top of the bed, located a pillow. She didn't even pull back the cover, but simply draped the edge of the comforter over her. On the other side of the bed, Garrett did the same.

Oh, and he turned away from her.

Good move. Lexie only wished she'd thought of it first. She wasn't afraid of the attraction. The energy. It was there, but there was something else brewing. Something that frightened her even more than the lust. It was all this shared camaraderie.

The parent connection.

It was potent stuff, and it was creating a weird sort of intimacy between them. And that couldn't happen.

She'd nearly ruined Garrett's life. Nearly cost him what he loved most. Lexie didn't need her memories to know she couldn't put him through that again. This time he was risking his career and his life to find their child. That was more than enough sacrificing for one man to make. No. There would be no sex. No intimacy. No emotional attachment. Because Garrett didn't want those things, and neither did she.

At the end of her little mental lecture, she hoped she'd convinced herself.

Nope.

She tested the idea, and the attraction was still there.

"We'll both need to be armed tomorrow. Carrying concealed, of course," she heard Garrett whisper, and she wondered if he was talking to her or to himself.

"Sounds good."

Garrett stayed quiet. The only sound in the room was his steady breathing and her pulse drumming in her ears.

"Worst case scenario," he continued a moment

later. He rolled over to face her. She didn't turn away. "If something goes wrong, we evade and escape."

She nodded. Stared at him.

Obviously uncomfortable, he stared back. Until his gaze drifted down a bit. She followed it and saw that her left breast had escaped her ill-fitting bra and was quite visible, since the neckline of her equally ill-fitting shirt had dipped off her shoulder. She quickly righted the problem.

"Sorry," she mumbled.

"Don't worry. I don't have the energy to react." But he immediately scrunched up his forehead. "Okay, there's no energy required for *that* type of reaction. I'm a man. That's all that's needed for a re-action." He mumbled some profanity. "But we aren't going there again, are we?"

"No."

Lexie tried to maintain eye contact, because it seemed the safest kind of visual exchange. But her gaze drifted down as well. No exposed chest for him. It was totally covered with a black T-shirt. But his arms were bare. No overly bulging muscles. Just toned and strong.

Welcoming.

But she wanted to pinch herself for allowing that last thought to pop into her head. However, she was right. His arms were welcoming. Heck, *he* was welcoming. Probably a by-product of that no-energy-required maleness. And it might have had something to do with this urge she had to move closer to him.

For comfort, of course.

"I know what you're thinking," he said, his voice a smoky drawl.

She certainly hoped not.

"Good thing the doctor said no sex," Garrett continued, obviously proving that he did indeed know what she was thinking. "And it's a good thing that we're exhausted. We need those kinds of obstacles, since we seem to be sort of mindless when it comes to each other."

"Yes, *mindless.*" That was the right word for it. "It's also stupid. We have so much on our plates right now."

"Primal lust doesn't care about that. Lust just wants us to act like bunnies so we can continue the human race."

"We've already done that," Lexie pointed out. "You'd think lust would be satisfied."

"It might never be satisfied," he mumbled.

In some ways, that sounded like a lifelong prison sentence. In other ways, it sounded like a challenge. "So, how do we counteract it?"

The corner of his mouth hitched. "Cold showers. Huge beds where you stay on one side and I stay on the other. And finally, I won't think about your breasts, and you won't think about…whichever body part of mine arouses you."

She laughed. She couldn't help it. Lexie didn't

remember at lot about this Garrett O'Malley, but she was quickly learning to appreciate his direct approach. Unfortunately, that appreciation also reminded her of why she'd had sex with him in the first place.

Which wasn't really a good thing to remember now.

She grabbed an extra pillow and put it between them.

"I forgot about physical barriers," Garrett told her. "That's a good way to counteract it. Pillows will make sure we don't bump into each other during the night."

Since that sounded far more interesting than it should have, Lexie decided it was time to say goodnight. She turned so that her back was to him. "Sleep tight, Garrett."

"Same to you." But he didn't fall asleep. "One more thing," he added. The smoke, heat and humor were gone from his voice. He was the cop now. "Tomorrow, we avoid confrontations that could lead to bullets flying. But it still might turn ugly. We might have to fight our way out of there. You understand that, don't you?"

"I understand."

It was abundantly clear. But even knowing she could be hurt, or worse, Lexie knew that wouldn't stop her.

In just a few hours, one way or another, she was going to that clinic to find their baby.

Chapter Eight

Garrett hated to rely on hope and a prayer, but he was hoping and praying that Lexie's disguise was good enough to keep them from being killed.

However, Lexie's newly tinted brunette hair and the heavy layer of makeup were at best a thin disguise. After all, no amount of makeup would hide her distinctive facial features, especially those unforgettable blue eyes. If the doctor or kidnapper were hanging around and got a look, their cover would likely be blown.

Lexie and he had dressed for the part. Garrett hadn't given up his jeans, but the T-shirt was gone. In its place was a white shirt and black leather jacket. Though it was summer in Texas, the jacket was necessary so he could hide his shoulder holster and Glock.

No jacket for Lexie. She was carrying her gun in her purse. Like him, though, she'd opted for jeans, but she'd discarded his shirt for a dressier one. It was blue, practically the same color as her eyes, and it fit her like a glove.

With the receptionist leading the way, Lexie and he walked down the massive cream-tiled hallway that would supposedly take them to the clinic director's office. They passed lots of people along the way. Some were pregnant women, their significant others, and then there were the staff members, who all wore blue or pink scrubs and seemingly permanent smiles. Many sported sunshine-yellow badges with comments like We Love Babies! and Babies Are Our Business!

Exclamation marks seemed to count on the badges, because each slogan had at least one.

Lexie walked beside Garrett. Shoulder to shoulder, holding his hand.

That, too, was part of the disguise.

They were playing the part of a loving couple in search of the perfect facility where they could have their first baby. If asked, Garrett would tell them that Lexie—or rather Erica, the fake name they'd chosen—was four months pregnant. And then he would ask lots of questions about doctors, the number of birthing rooms, etc. He'd do all of that while Lexie watched for the scumbags who'd taken their child and tried to kill her.

He felt Lexie's hand tense and grip harder. Garrett glanced around the corridor to see what had prompted that action. It wasn't a person, but a photo. Or rather a series of photos that lined both sides of the walls. The photos were of babies. Lots and lots of babies.

Garrett stared at her, wondering if she believed

one of those photos to be of their daughter, but then he saw the mistiness in her eyes. Her reaction had probably been spurred by the god-awful thought that their baby *wasn't* in the photos. Because someone at this birthing center had stolen her.

He gently squeezed Lexie's hand, hoping to convey that he was on the same page with her. The gesture seemed to surprise her. Her shoulders squared. A look of resoluteness replaced the mistiness, and she took her hand from his.

All right.

He was on the same page with her on that, as well. Distance was like a metaphorical pillow on a king-size bed. It wouldn't stop the intimacy from growing between them, but it would bring it to a temporary halt.

Just ahead of them, the receptionist stopped and opened one of the doors. "Dr. Blake, John and Erica Madison are here to see you."

"Show them in," a perky voice insisted. He could practically hear an exclamation point or two in it.

With all that perkiness, Garrett had expected the doctor to be very young and look like a debutante cheer-leader. But when Lexie and he went inside the office, they came face-to-face with a forty-something redhead whose smile didn't quite reach her ice-blue eyes.

"I'm Dr. Linnay Blake," she said in greeting. She gestured for them to sit in the cream-colored leather chairs across from her desk. "I'm the director here at the Brighton Birthing Center. Welcome. I'd be glad to answer any of your questions." She glanced down at her notes. "Erica, I understand you're in your fourth month?"

Lexie nodded and looked at Garrett, who took things from there. It was just as they'd rehearsed. Garrett wanted Lexie to speak as little as possible.

"That's right," he said in response to Dr. Blake's remark. "We know it's a little early to be visiting birthing facilities, but we want to be certain that we choose the right one. You see, my wife is very shy, and it might take her many visits to get comfortable with the facility and the staff."

Dr. Blake flashed another of those PR smiles. "That's not a problem. At Brighton, we welcome visitors and questions."

He hoped she meant that. "Will Erica and I be able to choose the obstetrician?"

"Absolutely. We have six here on staff." And with that, the doctor slid a glossy brochure their way. "Their bios are all in there."

Oh, but it wasn't just bios, Garrett soon learned. There were photos as well. Three men, three women. Lexie leaned over to study those photos with him. She was so close that she was touching his shoulder, and he felt her arm tense.

"Is there any one in particular you'd like to meet, sweetheart?" Garrett asked Lexie, using the best loving-husband voice he could manage.

"I don't want a female doctor," she said. She kept

her voice a raspy whisper. "And none of those men look very friendly."

"But I assure you they are," Dr. Blake insisted. "They're friendly and qualified to carry you through the entire process of prenatal care to childbirth. Here at Brighton, we want you to have the ultimate birthing experience."

Yeah. And sometimes that experience included baby kidnapping.

"A few months ago, I drove past the birthing center," Lexie continued, while trying to disguise her voice. "I saw a doctor in the parking lot. He was in his forties. Graying hair. He was tall and had wide shoulders. I had a very good feeling about him, and he's the doctor I'd like to use."

Lexie was describing the man who'd nearly killed her. Garrett didn't care much for the bold approach, but he liked Dr. Blake's reaction even less. Her smile faded, and her jaw quivered as she tried to force that smile back in place.

"I can't recall anyone of that description ever working here," the doctor explained. "He was a probably a visitor or someone interviewing for a position. We get a lot of applicants here at Brighton."

"I thought he worked here," Lexie insisted. She moved to the edge of her seat. "In fact, I'm certain of it. He was parked in a space reserved for employees only."

"Well, people don't always park where they're

supposed to park." Dr. Blake leaned back, away from Lexie, and pointed to the brochure. "Since you have very specific requirements for an obstetrician, perhaps you should take the brochure home and study the bios of our staff. I believe you'll find one who's suitable. If not, you're welcome to go elsewhere."

The doctor's tone had a don't-let-the-door-hit-you-in-the-butt ring to it. Lexie's questions had obviously made her very uncomfortable, and that was their cue to get out of there.

Garrett stood. "We'll read the brochure and have a look around on our own. If we decide to use Brighton, we'll let you know."

Lexie and the doctor stood as well, and Dr. Blake cast uneasy glances at both of them. "I'm afraid your *look around* will be limited to just this corridor and the reception area. I can't let you into the birthing areas. Privacy concerns, you understand."

Yes, but whose privacy did they want to guard?

Lexie and he stepped out of the room. Much to his surprise, no one was lurking in the hall to make sure they left the building. Probably because the security cameras were a human substitute. Someone was likely watching them, so the trick was not to draw attention to themselves. That might not be entirely possible, but it wouldn't stop him from trying.

They proceeded down the corridor. Even with the surveillance, Garrett intended to casually stroll as far as he could, perhaps even into the unoccupied birthing rooms, and he'd keep going until someone stopped them and escorted them back to the "safe" areas. They might get lucky and see something that would trigger Lexie's memory.

"Dr. Blake knows a lot more than she's saying," Lexie whispered. "That doctor was here, and she was covering for him."

"Maybe. Or maybe the doctor who delivered the baby was doing illegal things after hours. Maybe someone became suspicious, and Dr. Blake fired him. Now, she doesn't want his name associated with her perky, badge-sporting clinic."

Lexie nodded, but he could tell it wasn't a full-fledged agreement. "But even if that's what happened, Dr. Blake still knows who this doctor is."

"True, but there are ways to get that information. I can check IRS records. Well, I can have someone check them. Since I'm not supposed to be working on this case, it's best if I try to stay one step removed from the official part of the investigation. Going to the IRS would definitely qualify as official."

"So, other than a call to the IRS, what do we do?" Lexie asked.

"I'll set up that meeting with Billy Avery. In the meantime, we lie low, just beneath the radar, and we keep searching."

They stopped outside one of the rooms and tested the door. It was unlocked. So Garrett opened it. It looked like a homey bedroom, complete with a bassinet and other baby items. There was even a rocking chair.

"It's a recovery room," they heard someone say. A woman approached them along the corridor. "Most of our patients and their families are brought to rooms like this within minutes after delivery. We want the recovery period to mimic home life."

No doubt. But the bassinet was just another reminder that Lexie and Garrett didn't have their child. The room was a reminder that Lexie hadn't been given the royal treatment. Just the opposite. Instead of home life, she'd gotten hell.

"I'm Alicia Peralta," the woman said softly, shaking their hands. "I'm a nurse here at Brighton." She fired several nervous glances around the hall. "I heard you asking about that doctor."

Garrett and Lexie nodded and waited to hear what the woman had to say.

Alicia Peralta moved closer to them and came up on her tiptoes so she could whisper in Garrett's ear. "I know who the doctor is, and I know what he did. Come with me. It isn't safe to talk here."

LEXIE'S HEART WAS pounding, and it pounded harder with each step that Garrett and she took. They followed the petite, dark-haired nurse down the corridor that Dr. Blake had put off-limits, then made their way out a back exit that led to a parking lot.

Garrett and Lexie exchanged a glance, and he

slipped his hand inside his leather jacket, where his shoulder holster and his Glock were located. That only made Lexie's heart beat faster. Because if the nurse was leading them to an ambush of some sort, it would be devastating. But it wouldn't be nearly as devastating as not learning the information that would help them find their daughter.

"It should be okay to talk out here," Alicia said, taking them to a shady area at the back of the lot. No one was around. Well, no one Lexie could see, anyway. But she couldn't rule out the possibility of an attack, so she slipped her hand in her purse and curved her fingers around the small handgun that Garrett had loaned her.

"What do you know about this mystery doctor?" Garrett immediately asked.

Alicia turned her attention to Lexie. "I heard your description, and I think the man you're referring to is a former employee, Dr. Andrew Darnell."

Lexie almost cheered. Thank heaven. They finally had a name to go with the face that haunted her every dream, her every waking hour.

"Why didn't Dr. Blake volunteer this information?" Lexie asked.

"I think Dr. Blake realized that Darnell was using the clinic to recruit women for questionable adoptions. You see, we provide obstetrical services to a facility for unwed mothers that's just a few miles from here. I started to notice that most of those girls and young women were giving up their babies for adoption, and I think Dr. Darnell was somehow talking them into it."

"Or forcing them into it," Lexie mumbled.

Alicia stared at her. Nodded. "I suspect that could be true."

"What makes you say that?" Garrett questioned suspiciously.

"The records, for one thing. Many of Darnell's patients have missing or incomplete records. Plus, he had this habit of inducing labor at two or three in the morning, at a time when staff is usually at a minimum."

Was that what happened to her? Lexie wondered. Had she been at that facility for unwed mothers, and had Dr. Darnell been her obstetrician?

Had he taken her baby as part of some illegal adoption scheme?

As horrible as that theory was, there was a silver lining. Maybe her daughter was with a loving couple who was taking good care of her. Temporarily. Because Lexie intended to get her child back.

"Do you recognize me?" Lexie asked the nurse. "Was I a patient here?"

The woman studied her. "I don't think so."

"She normally has reddish hair," Garrett interjected.

Alicia continued to comb her gaze over Lexie's face. "You don't look familiar, but Dr. Darnell had a lot of patients that he saw on the side, after normal office hours."

Garrett had already suggested something similar.

If so, maybe Darnell was indeed acting alone, with his own henchmen and not clinic employees.

"Do you know how to contact Dr. Darnell?" Lexie asked.

"I'm sorry, I don't. I could ask around—"

"No," Garrett insisted. "I wouldn't want you to get in trouble."

And they didn't want anyone to get suspicious. Especially Dr. Blake, who might even be covering for the baby-stealing doctor.

Alicia nervously glanced around and checked her watch. "I have to get back inside before someone realizes I'm not at the nurses' station."

Without a goodbye, she hurried across the parking lot and slipped back into the center.

"You think she's telling the truth?" Lexie asked.

"Only one way to know." He pressed his hand to the small of her back to get her moving toward their unmarked police car, which he'd talked a friend at the SAPD garage into lending him. "I'll find out if this Dr. Darnell exists and if he worked here. If that checks out, then I can start looking into records at the home for unwed mothers."

"Illegal adoptions," Lexie stated, going over the possibilities. "How could it possibly go on here, at such a large clinic?"

"Where there's money to be made, people find a way. If Dr. Darnell was providing babies through private and perhaps illegal adoptions, it means that the birth families probably wouldn't have qualified for babies adopted through legal agencies. Maybe they didn't have the money for private legal adoptions, or maybe they couldn't pass the extensive background checks."

Her heart sank. Mercy! Her baby could be with people like that. Criminals, or worse.

"Don't go there," Garrett warned.

She looked up to see what had prompted his comment, and found him staring at her.

"Do not think worst case scenario here," he added. They got inside the car. "Just focus on what we have to do. One step at a time. And that first step is verifying what Alicia Peralta just told us."

Lexie nodded. "And we need to take a look at the home for unwed mothers."

"I'll send in a P.I. for that. If Dr. Blake is involved in this, she might have already alerted the home. Walking in there could be a trap."

He drove out of the parking lot and onto the rural highway that fronted the secluded birthing center. Both checked the mirrors, to see if anyone was following them, but they appeared to have the entire highway to themselves.

Garrett didn't waste any time. He snatched up his cell phone and pressed in some numbers. "I'm calling a P.I. friend. He's the best of the best."

"You're not going to get your brother involved in this?"

"Not yet. Not until I have something concrete." He paused. "Besides, I don't really want to have to explain to him why I took you inside a clinic where just three and a half weeks ago someone tried to kill you."

Garrett opened his mouth to say more, but his call must have connected. "Mason," he stated. "This is Garrett. I need a favor. Find out what you can about Dr. Andrew Darnell, Dr. Linnay Blake and a nurse named Alicia Peralta. They all worked or still work at the Brighton Birthing Center. I also need someone to get a personal look at a home for unwed mothers. I don't have an address, but it's located near Brighton."

It was exactly what they needed—information— and Lexie hoped it wouldn't take too long to get it.

Garrett ended the call and slipped his phone back into his pocket. "This P.I. works fast. We might have something as early as this afternoon."

The afternoon was only a few hours away. Not too long. Yet it seemed like a lifetime.

"How much trouble is this going to cause you?" she asked.

"Probably a lot."

There it was. That in-your-face honesty. Other times she appreciated it, but right now, it made her feel awful. "I really have this knack for ruining your career, don't I?"

He lifted a shoulder. "I'd have to be a heartless SOB to put a badge ahead of a baby."

That didn't answer her question. "But you didn't ask for this baby."

"Neither did you," he pointed out. "Making a baby is the risk any two people take when they have sex. Including safe, adrenaline sex."

She stared at him, frowned. "You're certainly being logical about all of this."

"You think so? Then you're wrong. It's a facade. There are too many things coming at us. The gunmen, the attraction, your memory loss, and the baby. I just keep thinking that if you hadn't heard her cry or if you hadn't managed to hold on to those few memories of the clinic and the doctor, we might never have known we had a daughter."

His words touched her in a way she shouldn't be touched. Because this shared empathy didn't mean all the problems they had were gone. No. Despite Garrett's response to the pressure, he still resented her. With reason. Old wounds didn't heal overnight.

"Just for the record, I don't expect you to forgive me," she told him. "And I'm not looking for a big-happy-family ending to all of this. I just want us to find our daughter."

His grip on the steering wheel tightened. "This doesn't look good," she heard Garrett say.

Confused, Lexie followed his gaze and saw that he was staring at the rearview mirror. She turned to glance behind them, and saw the SUV. It was obviously speeding on the country road, and it was closing in fast.

"It might not be one of the gunmen," she murmured, trying to reassure herself. But she reached for her gun.

Beside her, Garrett did the same.

Just as the SUV rammed into them.

Chapter Nine

The sudden impact nearly caused Garrett to lose control of the car. While he tried to keep a grip on his weapon, he clutched the steering wheel and somehow kept them from going into a ditch. He also pressed a tracking device and a security alarm that would alert headquarters. Backup would come.

Eventually.

But Lexie and he were out in the middle of nowhere, at least twenty miles from San Antonio, and it might take a half hour or more for backup to arrive.

That meant Lexie and he were on their own.

Hell.

He blamed himself for their situation. Even though they'd perhaps gotten critical information at the birthing center, that information might have a very high price tag.

It could get them killed.

Of course, doing nothing might cause them to lose their child, so he hadn't had much of an alternative.

"I can't see their faces," Lexie was saying.

Garrett cursed. "Stay down!" he ordered. The woman just didn't listen when it came to maintaining cover.

She did slip lower in the seat, but kept her head high enough that she could see out the side mirror. "I think there are three of them."

Three. The same number that had attacked them at his house. He didn't think it was a coincidence. No, these were likely the same three men. And if Lexie hadn't been in the car with him, Garrett would have figured out a way to get a better look at them. Maybe he could have even maneuvered into a direct, face-to-face confrontation, so he could beat these three senseless. But Lexie *was* with him, and he had to get her out of there.

The question was how.

The SUV slammed into them again. The car lurched forward, and Garrett clipped the edge of the ditch with his right front tire.

"I can shoot at them," Lexie insisted.

"And they can shoot at you," he countered.

There was another jolt from the SUV, and he heard the sound of metal tearing through metal, which likely meant the bumper was gone. At this rate, the much bigger and heavier vehicle could keep ramming them until the gunmen either ran them off the road or destroyed the car.

Except there was a third scenario.

And Garrett didn't immediately think of it—until a bullet slammed through the back windshield. The blast was deafening. No silencer this time, and the bullet tore through the windshield as well.

Another bullet quickly followed. Then another. Garrett fought to maintain control of the car, but the steering wheel gave an almost violent jerk. His stomach dropped to his knees. One of those bullets had ruptured a tire.

A dozen possible solutions went through his head, none of them good. And he cursed himself again for putting Lexie in this situation.

"What should I do?" she asked, her gun clasped in both hands.

Garrett didn't answer her, mainly because he didn't know how. It was time to do the evade and escape that he'd mentioned the night before.

There was another blast from a bullet. The Mustang jerked to the left. Another tire was gone, and within seconds, Garrett was driving on the metal rims. There was friction, smoke and the stench and shriek of steel slicing through the asphalt. They wouldn't last long like this, and he didn't think the gunmen planned to stop shooting anytime soon. He had to act fast if he had any hopes of getting out of this.

"Hold on," Garrett warned Lexie.

He twisted the steering wheel to the right and aimed at a path off the road. It wasn't much—barely six feet wide—and the car scraped between two scrub oaks. Garrett didn't stop. Didn't even slow down, though the lack of functioning tires was a hindrance. However, they weren't nearly as much of a hindrance as size was to the SUV. The driver behind him plowed into one of the oaks, bashing in the front end of his vehicle.

"They stopped," Lexie informed him.

He shoved her back down in the seat and fought to stay on the path. There was just one problem.

The path ended.

And directly ahead of them was a cluster of trees that would cause a deadly impact. Because he had no choice, Garrett slammed on the brakes.

"Undo your seat belt," he ordered Lexie. He took off his own belt, and at the same time opened his door. "Hit the ground running and stay ahead of me."

It wasn't the best of plans. Heck, it barely qualified as a plan at all. But at least his body might be able to block the bullets from hitting her.

Lexie did as he said. She jumped from the car and started to run. They didn't make it far before a bullet slammed into a tree right next to her head.

LEXIE'S LUNGS WERE burning, and it took a moment to realize she hadn't been shot, but she was in pain from the exertion caused by sprinting. Of course, the fear of dying didn't help calm her breathing, either. She felt on the verge of hyperventilating.

But not surrendering.

Garrett latched on to her arm and hauled her behind one of the sprawling oaks. He quickly pressed her back against the bark and moved in front of her. It was heroic, no doubt about it. He was willing to take a bullet, but that wasn't a smart thing to do. They had a much better chance of surviving this if they worked together.

"If we're back to back," she whispered, fighting for breath, "we can both return fire."

She saw the argument flash through his eyes, but she also saw the sound register. The sound of footsteps converging toward them.

"Move," she insisted. "It's the best chance we have."

When he didn't argue, Lexie stepped out, turned her back to his and aimed her weapon. And they waited.

The footsteps stopped.

Garrett lifted his head slightly, obviously listening. But either the gunmen had found some way to silence their movements or they'd left. But that was too much to hope for, so she stood there, her back against Garrett's. With every muscle in her body trembling.

He was rock solid, as if this was a normal part of his day. He didn't just wear a badge, he was a cop through and through. And Lexie was thankful for that. She needed him. Without Garrett, they might never unravel this case. Heck, without him, they might not make it out of these woods alive.

Who was behind this? Her former boss, Billy Avery? Or was it Dr. Darnell, the man who'd tried to kill her with that drug overdose? Of course, it might be neither. Dr. Linnay Blake had lied as easily as she'd smiled. Maybe she had something more to hide than her association with Dr. Darnell. Thank goodness the nurse had given them the man's name. Now they just had to find him and force him to tell them where their daughter was.

"I think they're gone," Garrett whispered.

"I think so, too." But just in case, she listened again for the footsteps that didn't come.

"We can't keep going through this," Garrett said, his voice bitter. "We need answers, and we need them now. Come on. We're getting out of here. I'm going to have a talk with Billy Avery."

Chapter Ten

Garrett waited until Lexie had excused herself and gone into the master bathroom of their temporary new home—a safe house. A few moments later, he heard her switch on the shower. Only then did Garrett turn to his brother for the talk he knew Brayden had been itching to have since they arrived at the safe house ten minutes earlier.

Brayden had been a godsend, Garrett silently admitted. After his brother had gotten the local sheriff out to the woods, the man had then driven Lexie and him to SAPD headquarters. Brayden had been waiting to take them to a safe house. Garrett welcomed the sanctuary in the sleepy San Antonio neighborhood, but he didn't welcome the flack he was about to get for what was essentially an unauthorized investigation.

"Don't start with a lecture," Garrett warned. He rifled through the bags of clothes and supplies. He smelled like sweat and trees and was in need of a shower. "If this had happened to one of your kids, you know you would have done the same thing that I did."

"Yes. But I would have done it with proper police backup. I might have even followed a few of the regs. I'm just funny that way."

Garrett rolled his eyes and shook his head. "We wanted to get to the clinic and find answers. We found them."

He located several pairs of jeans and a shirt, then waited a moment in an effort to gain control of his temper, his voice and his still-surging adrenaline. But gaining control was a battle he'd lose, he decided. He was pissed at himself and at anyone and everyone who could be behind this.

He turned and looked Brayden straight in the eye. "Every minute that passes is a minute Billy Avery or some other piece of slime could be using to hide my daughter so that I never find her."

"My daughter," Brayden repeated. He flexed his eyebrows. "That slipped out so easily that it sounds natural."

It had. And no one was more surprised than Garrett. "I don't know about it being natural. It's confusing. Terrifying. Frustrating." He scrubbed his hands over his face. "Life was a hell of a lot easier when I was just responsible for myself."

"But life isn't always about being easy."

Oh, man. Those words sounded like the start of something he didn't have the time or energy to hear.

"You're not about to launch into one of those big-brother speeches."

"No. I'll assume it's not required. Ditto for a lecture about you going into a dangerous situation without proper backup. I trust it won't happen again. Without a damn good reason, anyway."

With all the anger and emotion he'd been dealing with, Garrett had somehow forgotten that his big brother usually knew the exact thing to say. "Thanks."

"Don't thank me yet." Brayden folded his arms over his chest and shifted his stance. "I can't let you interrogate Billy Avery."

Hell. He'd obviously been too hasty in his exact-thing-to-say assessment. That wasn't the right thing to say, because seeing Avery could be vital.

"That kind of interrogation just isn't your forte," Brayden explained. "Not with all the personal stuff you have at stake. This requires a calm, objective head. I'll send in Katelyn."

Their sister was a sergeant in Homicide, and fellow officers called her "The Closer" because she was damn good at getting people to talk. Garrett couldn't argue with Brayden's decision to choose Katelyn over him.

Even if he really wanted to argue.

With his cruddy mood and fear of never finding his baby, he was more likely to physically assault Avery than he was to question him. That would go over really well with his lieutenant.

"I've checked all lines of communication at headquarters," Brayden continued. "I've questioned people. I've dug through surveillance reports and even tips from informants. And I can't find any involvement of a cop in this. I think the man who ran Lexie off the road was probably one of the gunmen dressed as a police officer."

Well, that was a relief, and it came at a time when Garrett needed some good news. *Any* good news.

"Oh, and one more thing," his brother added. "Lexie is now officially in your protective custody."

Of all the things that Garrett had anticipated he might say, that wasn't one of them. And Garrett wasn't entirely sure it qualified as more good news. Despite all the other stuff going on, Lexie and he still had this problem with lust.

"How'd you manage that?" he asked.

Brayden shrugged. "Someone shot into your house. They attempted to kill a police officer. That puts it under my umbrella of authority. And I say that during my investigation, Lexie is a critical witness. She needs police protection more than anyone I know. You seem the logical choice for that protection."

Garrett gave him a flat look. "Logical?"

Brayden smiled. "All right. Maybe not logical, but you're the most available."

Yes, he was. Plus he didn't want anyone else guarding her. Which made him...stupid. "Thanks again. I think."

"Well, you can repay me by not doing anything illegal. And by letting me help you."

There it was in a really ugly nutshell. *Help.* Garrett had issues with help. Mainly because he saw it as sign of his not being able to get the job done. But in this case, he welcomed the help from his brother.

"Stay here at the house," Brayden added. "I'll be in touch after Katelyn has interrogated Avery. And I'll arrange to have more clothes and a computer delivered in case you want to start doing some cyber research on Dr. Darnell and Dr. Blake." He headed for the door. "Note that I said cyber research, not the real thing. That *stay here* part isn't a suggestion."

Garrett only hoped it wouldn't be necessary to ignore it.

He double locked the door behind his brother, and because it might be years, if ever, before he felt he could keep Lexie safe, he checked out the window to make sure no one was lurking around. No one was there but his brother, who was already getting into his unmarked squad car. The street was quiet and empty. Garrett only hoped it stayed that way.

He took his phone from his pocket and was pressing in the number for the P.I. when Lexie came back into the living room. He got the P.I.'s voice mail and left a message to call him. It was overkill. If the man had any information, he would have already provided it.

Lexie walked closer to him, bringing with her the

scents of her shower, shampoo and soap. Garrett had never considered those smells to be particularly arousing, but they seemed to be doing the job now.

He took a step back.

Lexie wasn't exactly offering any erotic invitations. She wore jeans and a loose, dark blue, button-up shirt. His shirt. Probably because there hadn't been one for her in the bags. The SAPD had gotten Garrett's clothes from his house, but for Lexie, who had no house or belongings, the officer who'd assembled that bag had probably used whatever he or she could find around police headquarters.

Lexie had made use of all but one of the buttons, and there wasn't one bit of cleavage showing. Her hair was wet, most of the brown tint gone, and her face was still slightly beaded with moisture from the shower.

Okay, so that was erotic.

But since he was obviously a moron for lusting after her, it didn't count. She no doubt felt this steamy energy between them and planned to create a clothing chastity belt of sorts. Good for her.

"There's a cradle in the bedroom," she informed him.

Puzzled, Garrett went to the door that led to the master bedroom and bath. He glanced inside. Yep, there was a cradle tucked in the corner. "I doubt anyone arranged to have it here. Sometimes families have to use the safe houses, so it's probably been here awhile."

"I see." She tipped her head toward the second bedroom. "And there's no bed in there. It appears to be a storage room."

He hadn't known about that, either, but then this was his first time staying in a safe house. All other times, he'd merely dropped people off. But he understood her concern.

One bed.

Two people with no common sense or control.

"I'll sleep on the sofa," he assured her.

She nodded, visibly relieved. "One final thing— the shirt," she said softly, looking down at it. "It's yours, isn't it?"

"Yeah. But not to worry. It looks better on you, anyway."

And he was so sorry he'd said that.

Evidentially so was Lexie, because she stepped away and cleared her throat. "Any news about the investigation?" she asked. She adjusted the sleeves of the shirt.

"Some. A lot, actually. There doesn't seem to be any cop involvement in this. The guy who tried to kill you was probably just disguised as a cop."

"So, we can trust the police?" she asked cautiously.

"We can trust them." Garrett decided to give her the rest of the info checklist style—fast and without a lot of additional details. Some of it she'd like. One part of it she probably wouldn't. "Brayden's going to have a computer sent over so we can start checking on the doctors. My sister will be sent in to talk to Avery, and you're now officially in my protective custody."

Lexie blinked. "Oh."

She didn't have to elaborate on what had prompted that *oh*. Her uneasy expression said it all. Protective custody hadn't worked so well for them the last time.

He'd gotten her pregnant.

"It makes sense, I suppose," she said. "After all, we're stuck here together. It'll save your brother from having to assign someone else."

So she wasn't annoyed. Not exactly. But she sure didn't look pleased, either.

"Your brother seems like a nice guy." She adjusted the sleeve again, which didn't need adjusting, and walked past him into the kitchen. The house was small, and the living room was compact. That meant when she was passing through, they were close. Very close. And Garrett couldn't figure out why his body was noticing that.

"Brayden's a good cop," he said, to get his mind on business. He sank down onto the end of the coffee table. "Better than me, obviously. He wouldn't have nearly gotten you killed."

Lexie took a bottle of juice from the fridge, opened it and took a sip. She walked back into the living room and sat on the sofa directly across from him. Far enough away, but still close.

She started with a deep breath. "You saved my life today—again. I'd say that makes you a good cop, too."

Okay. It took a moment to find his voice. "That sounds like a compliment."

"It is." She paused, stared into her juice bottle as if what she was about to say would be difficult. "When I came to your house to confront you, I'd hoped that you would help, and you have. I couldn't ask for more than that."

That riled him a little. Mainly because she seemed surprised that he'd be interested enough to help her find their child. But Garrett decided to give her a break. The majority of his fellow officers probably thought he'd do pretty much anything to avoid fatherhood. And he had. Until fatherhood had hit him squarely in the face.

But now...

"Anyway, thank you," Lexie said, her voice hardly more than a whisper. She used the back of her hand to swipe at a tear, and she was probably hoping he hadn't seen it. "Sheez, I seem to be so weepy. Boohooing all over the place. I hate that. I hate everything about this."

So did he. And he hated the fact that Lexie, who wasn't a crier by nature, had been reduced to it. The tears were no doubt a sign of the deep pain she was feeling.

"You don't need to thank me," Garrett said. "And for the record, you deserve to have some boo-hooing time. You've been shot at twice, chased through the woods, and now what you're experiencing is a serious adrenaline crash. Even cops have trouble dealing with that."

"Oh, that's wonderful. An adrenaline crash. Postpartum blues. Memory loss. A big, gaping hole in my heart from missing my child." She shoved her damp hair away from her face. "I'm a mess, and I'm crazy for ever having doubted you. I can't believe I left your protective custody to go on the run. If I'd stayed, we wouldn't be in this nightmare. I created this, Garrett. I'm responsible for our daughter being missing."

Oh, hell. This wasn't just a heart-to-heart. This was a sprint down guilt lane.

"The person who took our baby is the one who created this mess," Garrett stated. "Not you. You left me because you had a darn good reason to leave."

But if she heard him, she certainly didn't acknowledge it.

"We've gone through so much," she continued. "Too much."

That was the truth, and it hurt. "We've got to go through a lot more," he murmured.

She blinked away the rest of the tears, obviously waiting for him to add to that. He almost said "and then what?" What would happen after they'd found their daughter? But Garrett wasn't sure he was ready to deal with the future. Not yet.

At best, he could hope that Lexie would be willing to share custody with him so he'd be a part of his daughter's life. At worst, she might take the child and run again.

Especially if she remembered why she'd left him in the first place.

Even though he hadn't wanted to rehash the past and the guilt right now, it was time she heard that reason. Time for him to confess all so she would know what a true jackass he was. He'd be damn lucky if she didn't throw something at him when he was done.

However, before he could speak, he heard her sob. Not a little one. And not a single tear sliding down her cheek. There were lots of them. Her breath caught, and the sound that escaped was one of pure torture. He would have to be a real ice man to be immune to that. So he pushed aside his confession, his concerns about the attraction. He pushed aside everything, reached out and did some pulling instead. He collected her in his arms and drew her to him.

She came willingly.

Maybe more than willingly.

Lexie seemed to melt against him, her body fitting so closely to his that he wasn't quite sure where he ended and she began.

"I couldn't do this without you," she whispered.

"And you shouldn't have to. We're partners in this. Parents," he amended.

"Yes." She sniffed back the tears and wiped her face. That parent reminder must have been what she needed to regain her resolve and her composure. "No more crying. I promise."

He hoped that was true, but the road ahead was going to remain bumpy. More crying was a distinct possibility.

"We have a plan," Lexie said, hiking up her chin. "We'll research the doctors and talk to Billy Avery. We'll find the man who took our baby. We'll win this."

Garrett looked down at her when she didn't say anything else. Not the brightest idea he'd ever had. Mainly because their mouths were close. Way too close. And then they got even closer. It took him a moment to figure out why. They were both at fault. Both obviously stupid. Because he dipped down his head, she leaned up, and their mouths met.

Just a touch.

Man, did it pack a jolt.

One taste of her, and he was on fire. He tried to hold on to what little logic his brain could produce. The logic that told him that kissing Lexie was not a good idea.

But other than his brain, the rest of him thought kissing her was a stellar idea. In fact, the rest of him thought it was absolutely necessary to take everything she was offering and more.

She hesitated a moment, probably because *her* brain was making the same argument as his. "How wrong is this?"

The answer was easy. "Really wrong."

Lexie seemed to consider that. And she shrugged. "To heck with it."

"To heck with it?" Garrett repeated, mentally groaning. One of them needed to play the responsible part here, and judging from what she'd said, it wasn't going to be Lexie.

"We've had a rough day," she argued. "This'll help."

No, it wouldn't. He knew it. She knew it.

But did that stop them?

Of course not.

She slid her arms around his neck. Garrett did some sliding as well. He hooked his arm around her waist and hauled her to him.

Logic went straight out the window.

He couldn't think. He didn't want to think. But, man, he could feel. Lexie's mouth was soft against his. And she tasted not like mint and tears, but like something hot and forbidden. Garrett decided that he'd take that taste over mint and tears any day.

Their tongues touched. It seemed to break down what few barriers they had left. The kiss became more than a simple taste. More than a simple act of passion. He took her mouth as if he owned it, and she didn't exactly resist the idea. She staked her own claim to *his* mouth.

Her breasts pressed against his chest, and the rest of their bodies began to adjust to the need that the kiss was igniting inside them. Almost frantically, they tugged at each other, and to further prove that he no longer had a logical thought in his head, Garrett pulled Lexie onto his lap.

She did her part to escalate what was happening between them. Her fingers went into his hair, dragging him closer. A lot closer. She slid her legs to cradle his hips. He held her hips as she moved forward, just as he did.

Garrett could have sworn he saw stars. Maybe even a constellation or two. The fit was mind-blowing, and her body seemed to welcome him. His body welcomed her, too, and he responded in the most basic male way. He got one heck of an erection, and even though his brain was still trying to urge him toward common sense, that erection had its own ideas.

So did he.

And what he wanted more than anything was Lexie.

Lexie had the same idea. She slid her hand between them, fumbling for his zipper.

Garrett knew one more move, and he'd be lost. Maybe forever.

Chapter Eleven

Garrett froze.

Lexie froze, too, wondering if someone was breaking into the safe house. With her heart racing and her body revved, it would have been difficult to hear something even that monumental. But though she lifted her head and listened, she couldn't hear anything alarming.

Until Garrett spoke.

"You're not supposed to have sex," he explained.

Oh, yes.

That.

That was indeed alarming. Because he looked so good and because she no longer just wanted him, she needed him. She ached for him. She tried to come up with an interpretation of the doctor's orders that would allow them to do what they both obviously wanted, but there wasn't even a loophole.

He glanced down at where their bodies were

pressed so hard against each other, and eased back. "Did I hurt you?"

She laughed. It was short-lived, more a laugh of frustration than humor. "You didn't hurt me." Lexie shook her head, moved off his lap and dropped back onto the sofa.

First there was the crying spell. Then the soul-baring conversation, where she'd admitted things that were probably best left unsaid. Of course, the reason she hadn't left them unsaid was because she wanted to have sex with him. It'd hit like a ton of bricks, or rather a ton of passion, when he'd tried to comfort her. The closeness. The way she felt in his arms. His scent.

Mercy.

That scent had her hormonal number.

Anyway, that's why she'd started to babble. Lexie figured if she talked until her jaw went numb she might not do something stupid—like kiss him.

"We just had one of those mindless episodes," she admitted, then paused. Tried not to continue to speak about yet more things best left unspoken. But her mouth didn't cooperate. "Was it always like that between us?"

"Always."

Something passed through his eyes. Regret, maybe? And he inched back, away from her. The passion they'd shared just seconds earlier seemed to evaporate, and the walls were back up between them.

Which was good.

They needed walls. Heaven knew they needed something. *Anything.* Because of her broken memories, she really didn't know him that well. Even though her body seemed to have no trouble remembering him.

"That was a mistake." She tried not to make it sound like a question.

It *was* a mistake. It had to be. The timing was lousy. Garrett and she were both exhausted from the stress and the uncertainty. That was it—the reason they'd responded as they had.

And Lexie was almost certain she believed that.

He got up and went into the kitchen to retrieve a bottle of water. "I've made a lot of mistakes with you."

His comment sounded like more than wall-erecting. It was the comment of a man who felt guilty. Not just about kissing her, either.

"We're not going through that whole thing about you nearly getting me killed, are we?" she asked rhetorically. "Because I nearly got you killed by coming to your house. If you're keeping score, that makes us even."

"No. It doesn't."

Lexie huffed and decided it was time to nip this in the bud. "I won't let you beat yourself up. I know that kiss pushed limits." She winced. Even she couldn't downplay it that much. "Okay, so it was more than a kiss, and it didn't just push limits. It bulldozed them. That's still no reason for you to feel guilty."

"Oh, yeah?"

"Oh, yeah," she countered. "You've done everything you possibly could to keep me at arm's length. And to keep me alive." She knew she was babbling again. Why couldn't she stop? Hoping for a truthful, hasty conclusion to this babblefest, Lexie said, "You're a good cop."

"Many wouldn't agree." He answered so easily, so adamantly, that it was clear someone had convinced him that he didn't qualify as a good cop.

She didn't know who these naysayers were, but she didn't care much for them. "Then those *many* are wrong. I've been with you, Garrett. I've watched you work. You're very good at what you do."

He stared at her. "You don't remember me telling you much about my family, do you?" He didn't wait for her to answer. "My folks are retired cops. Both highly decorated. My mom collared a serial killer when she was a rookie, and she wasn't even working Homicide. Dad has an entire desk filled with awards because he had an eerie knack for saving people. Brayden was the youngest cop at headquarters to make lieutenant. Katelyn was the youngest female to make sergeant."

Lexie shrugged, unsure of where this was leading. "You obviously come from a family of high achievers."

"Yeah, and I'm not one of them."

Lexie almost babbled again. She almost voiced the argument she'd already expressed—that he was very good. But Garrett needed to get things off his chest.

"When there's a hostage situation, they call in Brayden. Calm under pressure. Smart. He could negotiate with Satan—and win," Garrett continued. "And my sister, Katelyn—she's the one you want in an interrogation room to get a legitimate confession. Me? I'm the one they ask to kick in doors of crack houses."

So this was where it was leading.

"If the doors aren't kicked down, the cops can't get inside to arrest the bad guys." Lexie went to him, grabbed his chin and forced eye contact. "If you're trying to warn me of your shortcomings, don't bother. Because you see, you've got something your siblings and your parents don't have. You have a child out there, and your desire to find her makes you the perfect man for the job."

He stared at her. And stared. By degrees, she saw her words truly sink in. "Thanks for the reminder. And I won't let you or our baby down. No failing this time."

He stepped away from her and picked up a notepad and pen from the counter bar that divided the living area from the kitchen. "We have too many things we need to be working on, and kissing and whining about accomplishments aren't on the list."

He didn't wait for her to challenge that. Nor did he give her a moment of regret for the kisses they weren't likely to share anytime soon. He wrote Dr. Darnell's name across the top of the page. "He's the key to finding our baby."

"I agree." And seeing Darnell's name was the

exact jolt of reality Lexie needed. "Because even if Billy Avery is behind this, Dr. Darnell could be working for him. Plus, I have no doubts that the doctor knows where our baby was taken."

Garrett wrote Billy Avery's name beneath Dr. Darnell's, staring at the paper as though hoping the answers would simply appear. Lexie tried to force some answers into her brain as well. She focused on the two men and willed herself to remember any clues that might be hidden in her broken memories.

And she saw something.

Not Avery or Dr. Darnell. What she saw was Garrett. Naked. Of course, she'd seen him naked the night she broke into his house and held him at gunpoint. But this was different.

She was naked in his arms, and they were tangled around each other. On a coffee table in a hotel room.

"What's wrong?" Garrett asked.

Lexie blinked hard to force away those images, but they stayed, right there in front of her.

"You're breathing hard," he pointed out. "And you look flushed."

Oh, she didn't doubt either of those things. The images were so real that she could feel him inside her. Every inch of him.

And sweet mercy, it felt good.

He hadn't been gentle. She hadn't wanted that from him. She'd wanted him. Then. There. Immediately. And he'd accommodated her.

"What's wrong?" he repeated.

"Nothing." Though how she'd managed to answer him was a mystery.

"Did you remember something else?" Garrett demanded.

She shook her head. "Nothing important."

"The expression on your face tells me differently."

He obviously wasn't going to let this drop, but Lexie figured it wasn't a good idea for them to discuss sex. Not after that mind-blowing kissing session and their resolution to dig for the truth.

"The memories are trickling in," she explained. She paused. Cleared her throat. "At least I think they're memories. About us."

Sheez, she hoped they weren't fantasies.

"Tell me," Garrett insisted. Though he didn't look exactly pleased about rehashing this. "I'll let you know if it really happened."

Lexie decided it was best to confess as quickly as possible. "A coffee table. A hotel room. You and me. You have a small dragon tattoo on your left shoulder."

She wouldn't mention the matching one on his toned left butt cheek.

He waited a moment that seemed an eternity, then nodded. "It's real. The tattoos are relics of a wild and crazy weekend I spent with my brother in Mexico. There was lots of tequila involved."

Okay. So that part was confirmed. "And the rest is real as well?"

"I can guarantee it."

Wow. That gave her a lot to think about, especially since the memories just kept coming.

And she felt herself near the breaking point.

Thankfully, the memories broke up. She saw snippets of the two of them dressing. There was a phone call. For her.

"I started crying," she said.

"Yes." His voice sounded different, and she lifted her eyes to meet his. "Because you found out that your father had died."

Lexie's breath shattered and pain stabbed through her heart. Her father. He'd been frail for years, left that way after a stroke. But he'd been alive and in a nursing home. He'd been a part of her life.

Until that day.

The memories came like bullets. Hitting her. Hurting her. "You knew my father was dead?"

"Yes. And I didn't tell you."

Lexie had just enough of the memories to fill in the blanks. "You didn't tell me because I would have been too upset to testify. You kept his death from me."

She moved away from him. As far as she could get. Because it hurt as if it the wounds were fresh.

"Your testimony would have assured a conviction," Garrett admitted. "And I put that above what you needed to know—that your father was dead."

Lexie nodded frantically. "That's why we argued. That's why I left."

"That's why you left."

She waited a moment. Her hands were trembling now. She figured it wouldn't be long before all of her was trembling. "I need some time," she managed to say, and she started toward the bedroom. She intended to go inside and duck under the covers for a while. She needed to think about this, to sort it all out.

But the phone rang, just as it had in her memory.

Garrett glanced at her. It seemed as if he was going to say something, but instead, he turned and pressed the speaker function on the phone. "O'Malley."

"It's Mason Tanner," said the man on the other end of the line.

It was the P.I. Garrett had hired, and Lexie knew her grieving and pain would have to wait. This call could be critical.

"What do you have for us, Mason?" Garrett asked.

"I found Dr. Andrew Darnell. He's living in an upscale neighborhood just off the intersection of San Pedro and Highway 1604. I think Darnell's your man. I haven't been able to dig too deep yet, but I'm positive he's up to his neck in illegal adoptions."

Lexie gave up trying to force her legs to support her. She leaned against the bedroom door.

"Define illegal."

"From just the preliminary stuff, he seems to be involved in providing very wealthy clients with speedy adoptions. These clients pay him lots of money for healthy infants, and I don't think the good doctor cares much if the birth mothers voluntarily participate in his project. In fact, I think he's using a women's shelter and several homes for unwed mothers as his own personal baby farms."

It took Lexie a moment to process the information. "So, the children aren't being harmed?" she asked.

"No way. Darnell's clients want healthy, well cared for babies. It's my guess that if he has your daughter, then she's being treated like royalty."

Unlike the way the doctor treated the birth mothers. God, how many had he killed or tried to kill? Lexie probably wasn't the first. Nor would she be the last, unless they did something to stop him.

"How long before the babies go to the adoptive parents?" Lexie asked.

"I've only traced one paper trail. It was for a newborn boy six months ago, and it took Darnell about a month to place him with his new family."

A month. Since their baby was already three and a half weeks old, that didn't give them much time. A week at best. And it broke her heart to have to admit that it might already be too late. Her baby might have already been adopted, and if so, it could possibly mean a lengthy investigation and a legal battle to get the child back from the adoptive parents. Still, she couldn't dwell on that. She had to focus on what she could control, and getting the truth out of Darnell was a real possibility.

"I'm having my staff go through as many of Darnell's records and computer files as we can get our hands on," the P.I. continued. "My advice? Don't ask how we came across these files. I've tried to preserve the originals in case they're needed for evidence. But there's a possibility they won't be admissible. I didn't think you'd want me to wait around until Darnell finds a way to hide or destroy them."

"You did the right thing," Garrett assured him. "I'd like copies of those files."

"I'll have someone courier them over. Might not be today, though. I think we're getting close. If there's anything to find in these files, we'll find it. I'll also arrange to have someone put Darnell under surveillance."

"I'll handle surveillance," Garrett insisted.

The P.I. paused. "You think that's wise?"

Garrett made a sound of frustration. "I have to do something, Mason. I can't let that SOB give our child to someone else."

"That's what I thought you'd say. Be careful."

"I will." Garrett reached for his shoulder holster and weapon. "We need a rental car," he said to the P.I. "That way, I don't have to wait around for the department to issue me another unmarked vehicle." He looked back at Lexie. "Get your shoes."

But she was one step ahead of him. "I'm going with you to Darnell's."

"Absolutely. I can't leave you here by yourself. Hurry," he added.

Garrett lowered his voice and said something else to the P.I.

Something about her father.

She nearly stopped the shoe search to ask what that was all about, but time was critical.

If they didn't find Darnell right away, then they might never see their child.

Chapter Twelve

"That's Darnell's house," Lexie verified, checking the address that the P.I. had given them.

Garrett parked their car just up the street, so that Darnell's front door and garage were visible in case the doctor spotted them, got suspicious and tried to run. They had already made sure he was home. Pretending to be a telemarketer, Garrett had called the house, and Dr. Andrew Darnell had taken the call.

"I want to bash in his door," Garrett grumbled.

"I wouldn't mind doing some bashing myself," Lexie concurred. She was fidgeting. Checking her gun. Rechecking it. "Do you think he has the baby in there with him?"

"It's possible, but doubtful. Darnell would probably want to be one step removed from the evidence that could get his butt arrested."

But there was no mistake—one way or another, Garrett intended to arrest the man, and he would do whatever it took to get a full confession. That confession would include telling them the whereabouts of the baby.

"I can't just sit here," Lexie informed him.

"You might not have a choice. He might recognize you."

Another gun check. "So, what do we do?"

It was the million dollar question. Garrett had gone through several possible scenarios, and he didn't like any of them.

"We wait about a half hour until it's dark," he told her. "And then I have a look around his house. Well, I'll look through his windows, anyway. I'll check to see if he's armed. Make sure he's alone. If he is, then I'll ring the doorbell, introduce myself and have a little chat with him. I want to hear what he has to say, since I'm pretty sure Darnell is the right man."

"So am I. I'm almost positive that I remember the other man saying his name that night when I gave birth."

Good. Those were exactly the kinds of memories they needed. It was enough to validate whatever he had to do to get Darnell to confess.

Garrett shifted in the seat so he could make eye contact with her. "What else do you remember about that night?"

"About the delivery…I've recalled a few things. Not so much about the days following it. But the blanks are filling in, and it seems as if every hour I remember something else."

"Like the coffee table," he commented. Best to leave out the whole sex incident on that coffee table. "And, of course, you remember that I'm a jerk for not telling you about your father."

She dodged his gaze and looked out the window. She also dodged his comment. "I went into labor at the home for unwed mothers. I was staying there because money was tight, and I didn't want to tap into my bank accounts because…well, just because."

"Because you thought I'd find you." Ironic. While she was worrying about him finding her, he hadn't even been looking. Because he had no clue that she was carrying his child. The SAPD had been searching for her, but only because she was a missing material witness. Their search had had nothing to do with what had happened personally between Lexie and him.

"Someone at the home took me to the Brighton Birthing Center," she continued. "And Dr. Darnell was there. He gave me something, to speed up the labor, he said. The pains started coming fast, and I didn't even have time to catch my breath before another one started."

This was hard to hear. Mainly because he could almost feel what she'd been going through. Alone. Frightened. In labor. And Darnell had taken full advantage of that.

"The baby came," she continued. "And I had this overwhelming feeling of…love. I wanted to hold her, but then the other man came in. He took her, and that's when Darnell gave me that shot."

Garrett wished he could go and undo that. Not just the shot, but everything Lexie had been through. "Did Darnell say anything when he gave you the drug?"

"Only that I needed some rest." She shook her head. "I didn't want to rest. I wanted to hold my baby, and the other man was wrapping her in a blanket. That's when he called Darnell by name. I knew he was about to take the baby away, but everything seemed out of focus, and I was dizzy. I tried to push Darnell away and get out of the delivery bed, but he held me down. I had to do something, so I pretended to pass out. It worked. Darnell left the room. I got up and went to find the baby."

"I wish I could have been there to help." If he had been, that goon wouldn't have gotten out of the room with their child. And Lexie wouldn't have had to go through hell. "I'm sorry."

"Yes. Me, too." She reached out and touched his chin. "There's no need for you to beat yourself up about any of this. I left you of my own accord."

"You left because I gave you no choice."

"Oh, I had choices, Garrett, and just like you, I didn't make very good ones. I loved my father, and I didn't handle his death well. I didn't handle a lot of things well."

He wasn't going to let her beat herself up, either. "Hey, I had sex with an adrenaline fatigued, highly stressed witness who was in my protective custody. Talk about crossing lines. Breaking rules. Doing impulsive things."

"I think that's what I like about you."

"You *like* me?"

"Parts of you, anyway." She actually blushed. Smiled. "I keep trying to imagine going through this investigation with your brother. All that logic. All that calmness. After an hour or two, I'd want to scream."

"You don't want to scream with me?" he asked jokingly.

"Oh, I still want to scream. For a lot of reasons. Including the things that drove us apart."

Yes. There was always that. "And that kissing, groping session didn't help."

"No. But I think we're driven by Mother Nature, or simply hormones, when it comes to this weird attraction. We're in our prime reproductive years, and I was obviously ovulating during the coffee table incident."

So, the attraction was just physical. Garrett gave that some thought and decided she was probably right. Mere attraction. A fire so hot that they'd tried to burn it up with a round of sex.

"But if that's true, why do I still want you?" Garrett asked.

"Because we're connected with this camaraderie over finding our child?" She paused. "Or because we still have the hots for each other?"

"Or both." Though he liked the second option

best. Lust. Plain and simple. He could deal with that, especially since he already had so much to deal with. He needed to figure out how to be a father, and maybe then he could figure out how Lexie fit into his life.

It was entirely possible that she didn't want to fit.

During the time she'd been in his protective custody, she'd said several times that she wasn't the relationship type. She'd had a failed engagement and just didn't see herself fitting into a traditional role. So that meant they'd have to work out some kind of nontraditional shared custody arrangement—whatever that was.

First, though, they had to find their baby.

Garrett glanced around them. The streetlights had popped on. It was time to get to work and do some close surveillance of Darnell.

"Stay put," Garrett advised Lexie. "If something goes wrong, call my brother for backup."

She checked her gun again. "You think something will go wrong?"

It was a distinct possibility, but Garrett kept that to himself. "Everything will be okay. Once I've verified that Darnell is alone, I'll go in and have a chat with him."

The words had hardly left his mouth before the doctor's garage door opened. A lanky man walked around the back of a black sports car.

"That's him," Lexie verified.

"You're sure?"

"Positive."

Dr. Darnell had a rather large suitcase in his hand. He opened the trunk and placed it inside. He glanced around—the kind of glance a person made when he was checking to see if he was being watched. But if Darnell noticed them, he certainly gave no indication of it.

"He's leaving," Lexie said, lowering her voice to a whisper. "We have to stop him." She reached for the door handle, but Garrett clamped his hand over hers.

So, it was decision time. They could follow the doctor, see where he was going. But maybe he was going to the airport, where he could slip away and never be seen again. That was too huge of a risk to take.

"I'd rather you stay here," Garrett said.

But he was talking to the air, because Lexie was already out of the car. Thankfully, she kept her gun tucked away in her waistband. He figured that was best, since they were going to attempt to talk to Darnell. If bashing or shooting was required, Garrett would be the one to do it.

He hurried out of the car and caught up with her. Grabbing her arm, he positioned her behind him as they made a beeline for the doctor. Darnell must have detected some sound or movement because he whirled to face them. His hand went in the direction of his jacket.

"Don't," Garrett warned. To make his point, he pulled back his own leather jacket so he could flash his Glock and the badge he had clipped to the waist of his jeans. Both certainly got the doc's attention. His watery gray eyes widened. "Going somewhere, Dr. Darnell?"

"Not that it's any of your business, but I'm leaving for my vacation. Now, who are you, and what the hell do you want?"

"I'm Sergeant Garrett O'Malley, SAPD. And what I want is information. I'm going to ask questions, and you're going to answer them."

He volleyed uneasy glances from Garrett to Lexie. "Am I under arrest?"

"That'll all depend on your answers."

He turned to finish putting the suitcase in the trunk. "If I'm not under arrest, then you can contact my attorney. He'll answer those questions."

Lexie stepped out from behind Garrett, much to his frustration. She basically put herself in the line of fire. "Remember me?" she asked. "Because I remember you. You tried to kill me."

Darnell looked at her. And dismissed her. "I have no idea what you're talking about. I've never seen you before in my life."

"Liar. I want to know where you took our baby."

Now, there was a reaction. The icy facade melted in a puddle of exposed nerves.

"I want names," Garrett insisted. "I want the location of our baby. And I want those things now."

Garrett detected some movement from the corner

of his eye. He made a split-second assessment to determine that it wasn't Lexie.

It wasn't.

The hulk of a man came right at them. He easily outsized Garrett by sixty, maybe seventy pounds. Garrett went for his gun, but it was too late. The man launched himself into the air, tackling them. All but Darnell went sprawling onto the concrete floor of the garage.

Garrett tried to push Lexie away so that she wouldn't get hurt, while at the same time trying to retrieve his gun. The guy had different plans. He backhanded Lexie, then bashed his fist into Garrett's jaw. A second later Garrett registered the metallic taste of his own blood.

That really pissed him off.

Not his blood. Not even the fist in his jaw. But the fact that this jerk had slapped Lexie.

Garrett heard a feral growl come from his own chest, and he somehow flipped the man off them. It was time to do his own launching, and he went right after the guy, and didn't spare his fists.

"Darnell's getting away," Lexie shouted.

Garrett heard the car engine start. He glanced up and saw that she was going after the doctor, but he also noticed something else. With Lexie's position, Darnell would likely run her over.

Because Garrett's attention was diverted, the hulk got in a wicked right hook. Garrett ignored the pain that slammed through him, and scrambled away from the guy. He gripped Lexie's shoulder and dragged her out of the way just as Darnell gunned the engine.

His car screamed out of the garage, leaving the stench of burning rubber. But Garrett couldn't watch him drive away. He had a more immediate problem. The hulk was reaching for a gun, no doubt intending to shoot them.

Garrett beat him to the punch.

He drew his Glock and aimed, and even though he preferred to keep the guy alive, he was willing to shoot to kill. He must have conveyed that with his glare, because the big man lifted his hands in surrender.

"Darnell got away," Lexie said, the frustration in her voice obvious. "We need to go after him."

Garrett couldn't. It was too huge of a risk with Lexie's life. And he'd already put her in mortal danger tonight. Best not to repeat that. Plus, going after Darnell would mean letting this big woman-slapping thug go. The guy would likely come after them, and if Garrett took the time to tie him up, Darnell would be long gone, anyway.

"Call for backup," Garrett told her. "We'll get this slime to headquarters for questioning."

"But Darnell—"

"There'll be an APB on him. They'll find him. I promise."

Garrett couldn't guarantee that promise, but he knew one thing for sure. One way or another, Darnell's hired gun was going to give them answers.

Chapter Thirteen

Lexie couldn't take her eyes from the video feed on the computer screen. Why, she didn't know. Dr. Darnell's bodyguard wasn't saying a word. In fact, the only thing he'd said in the past hour was that he wanted his lawyer. A call had been made, and the lawyer had arrived. The bodyguard still hadn't issued one comment.

"I want to go to headquarters," Garrett mumbled. "I want to talk to this guy."

Lexie wanted the same thing. The problem? Garrett's brother, Brayden, had ordered them to stay away. And he'd meant it, too. Both Garrett and she were just too emotionally involved in the case to do anything rational. Brayden was right. Garrett wanted to beat the information out of the guy, and Lexie probably would have assisted. She could still feel the sting of the guy's hand on her face, but the worst sting of all was the pain in her heart.

"Maybe they'll find Dr. Darnell," Lexie said. The

police had to find him. Or maybe they'd find something in his house—especially since the baby obviously wasn't there. Darnell's house was yet another place they'd been ordered not to go. Brayden had said it would compromise the investigation, that any evidence found there might be considered tainted simply because Garrett and she were in the vicinity.

So they had returned to the safe house, and the only consolation was that Brayden had arranged for them to receive video feed of the bodyguard's interrogation.

For all the good that'd done them.

They were at a standstill.

Or were they?

Lexie grabbed the phonebook and located the number of the Brighton Birthing Center.

"Mind telling me what you're doing?" Garrett asked.

"I'm calling the clinic director, Dr. Linnay Blake. I want to know why she lied to us when she said no one fitting Dr. Darnell's description had ever worked there."

"Good idea. You want me to talk to her?"

Lexie shook her head, pressed in the number and turned on the speaker function so that Garrett could hear. She got the receptionist, who asked her to hold, that Dr. Blake would be on the line shortly. "I'd rather not pull any punches with her if you don't mind."

"Go for it," Garrett agreed. "I'm all for anything that will get this investigation moving in our favor."

"Dr. Blake," the woman answered. "How may I help you?"

"I'm Lexie Rayburn. My friend, Garrett O'Malley, and I were at Brighton Clinic yesterday, and you lied to us. You said Dr. Andrew Darnell had never worked there, but I know for a fact that he did."

"I'm not sure what you mean." Dr. Blake sounded convinced of it, too.

Lexie, however, obviously wasn't convinced. "You know exactly what I'm talking about, probably because SAPD has already contacted you to set up an interview."

"What do you know about all of this? What do they want?"

"They want to know why Dr. Darnell and you are up to your necks in illegal adoptions."

"But I'm not. I had nothing to do with any of that."

"So, why lie?" Lexie demanded.

There were several long seconds of silence. "Because I was scared. Look, I don't know what's going on, but I asked Dr. Darnell to resign when I got complaints that he was pressuring women from the shelter and the home to give up their babies for adoption."

"And you didn't think to turn this information over to the police?" Garrett asked.

"I couldn't. I got these letters. Probably from Dr.

Darnell, though he didn't sign them. They were threats that if I didn't stay quiet, something bad would happen to me."

"I want to see the letters," Garrett insisted.

"I shredded them."

"Oh, that's convenient."

The doctor gave an audible huff. "Look, I don't know what you're accusing me of, but I'm the victim here. I had my life threatened when I tried to do the right thing."

"The right thing would have been going to the police with your suspicions about Darnell," Lexie pointed out.

"As far as I know, he hadn't done anything illegal. Pressuring women into adoption is unethical, but there was no reason to get the cops involved."

"They're involved," Garrett assured her. "And you're going to be one of their prime suspects in the disappearance of a baby girl who was born three and a half weeks ago."

"What baby?" Dr. Blake demanded.

Lexie was getting so tired of the denials. Either Linnay Blake was putting on a good act or else she truly was innocent. "A baby that Dr. Darnell had kidnapped so he could use her for an illegal adoption."

"I didn't know. I swear I didn't know."

"Well, someone there did," Lexie countered. "Someone had to have assisted him."

"Not me. I wouldn't do anything like that. I love

children. Look, I don't have any proof, but if you're looking for suspects, look at Alicia Peralta, a nurse who works here at Brighton."

That sent Lexie searching Garrett's eyes. "Why her?" she asked, skeptical of what she might hear.

"Because she quit her job this morning. No notice. No explanation. When I got to work at nine, her resignation was on my desk."

That could mean nothing other than the fact that Alicia Peralta was scared. Maybe she'd even gotten some threatening notes. Of course, the flip side was that the nurse could be guilty. But if she was, why had she told them about Dr. Darnell?

"Where would Dr. Darnell have taken the baby that he stole?" Garrett asked.

"I have no idea."

"Then think of one," he demanded. "Think of any and all possibilities."

"Maybe his house?"

"Not there. Try again."

"I don't know. I honestly don't." Her denial sounded frantic and tearful. But were either of those emotions sincere? "Dr. Darnell and I weren't close. We rarely had contact with each other."

Garrett moved closer to the phone. "Think hard and try to figure out where he would have taken that baby. Because you see, the police might not think you're innocent, and information like that might be a good bargaining chip that'll keep you out of jail."

With that warning, Garrett ended the call.

He scrubbed his hand over his face and groaned. "Hell. I feel like we're running around in circles."

"Well, we're better off than we were two days ago," Lexie decided. "We have a suspect, and the police are looking for him. Plus, his bodyguard might talk."

"Yeah, maybe."

"There are also Dr. Darnell's files and computer records that the P.I. copied. Those should be here sometime before morning. We can go through them and maybe find something."

She hoped. And right now, hope was all they had. Oh, and they had each other. That shouldn't have given her much comfort, but it did.

Garrett sank down on the sofa next to her, and as if it was the most natural thing in the world, pulled her into his arms. Mercy, it felt good to be there. It felt even better to lean on someone.

It also felt dangerous.

Like something they should be trying to avoid. Except she could no longer remember why avoidance was necessary.

Oh, yes.

His badge. Another personal involvement with her wouldn't do much to help his career. And there was that whole issue of how she would feel about him when her memory fully returned.

"What are you thinking about?" he asked.

She nearly dodged the question. And probably

should have. But after all they'd been through, it seemed pointless to keep her thoughts to herself. "I was wondering how I would feel about you when my memories fill in."

He looked ready to dodge it as well, but he didn't. "Are you still furious with me because I didn't tell you about your father's death?"

"No."

"Well, you should be."

"You're a cop. It was the cop thing to do. Which only proves, of course, that you're on the same high-achieving level as your family."

"No. It proves that I put my badge above all else." He waited a moment before he continued. "Besides, when you get back all of your memories, you may realize that you hate me. That might be the real reason you walked out. The news about your father might have only been the last straw that sent you running."

"Why would I hate you?" she asked.

"Because I'm pigheaded."

He mumbled a few other derogatory adjectives. Temperamental. Obsessed. All semi-true. His outpouring seemed to drain him of his common sense or something, because he leaned in and kissed her. It wasn't frantic and hot, and it didn't seem like foreplay. It was like his embrace—natural. And if he had any motive or expectations beyond that one kiss, he didn't act on them.

Lexie did.

Well, she didn't exactly act, but she did have a revelation of sorts. An uncomfortable one. It was the one thing Garrett didn't need to hear: she was falling for him all over again.

Which either made her stupid, or made her suspect he was her soul mate.

Maybe both were true.

"Cuddling probably isn't a good idea," she mumbled. But she didn't move away. She darn sure didn't want to get up and go into another room, where she'd be alone. Alone was the last thing she wanted right now.

"I wouldn't want this to get around to my poker buddies, but cuddling is almost always a good idea."

She smiled. "It's foreplay," she contradicted.

"It can be. But for us, breathing is foreplay."

Lexie couldn't contradict that.

"You walk into the room," he continued, "I smell your toothpaste and I'm aroused."

So, that's what did it for him. Toothpaste. "The thought of your tattoo arouses me. Not the one on your shoulder. The one on your butt."

As if this was the most mundane conversation in the universe, he nodded. "You remember that one?"

"Yes. And I remember your butt. Hence the part about me getting aroused." But it did make Lexie wonder where this dialogue—and the passion she felt—were going. "Something this intense burns out quickly."

"You bet," Garrett agreed. But he sounded as if he was questioning it as much as she was.

Lexie definitely wasn't convinced. "So after we've found our daughter, what stops us from having another round on the coffee table?"

He looked down at her. "Nothing. Except us, of course."

She rolled her eyes and groaned. They weren't going to stop anything sexual. Even now, less than a month after giving birth, she wanted him—bad. Still, this could easily be a too fast, too hot situation. It might take them hours of time on the coffee table to realize that they weren't compatible.

But even she couldn't deny that it'd be fun.

A ringing sound blasted through the room, and it took Lexie a moment to figure out it was coming from Garrett's cell phone. He practically leaped off the sofa and hurried to his jacket to retrieve it.

"O'Malley," he answered.

Within seconds, his expression changed completely, going from extreme anticipation to surprise. Maybe even shock.

"I'm very interested in what you have to say," Garrett commented to the person on the other end of the line.

"Who is it?" Lexie whispered.

"Dr. Andrew Darnell. He's ready to talk."

Chapter Fourteen

"Where are you?" Garrett asked Darnell. "Maybe we can have this conversation face-to-face?"

"Not yet. Not until we get a few things straight. Then I'll gladly meet with you."

Lexie hurried over, and because she was several inches shorter than Garrett, she stood on the coffee table in order to put her ear next to his.

"I'm listening," Garrett assured him. And he silently cursed because there was no way to record this conversation. He only hoped that didn't come back to haunt him.

"I know you have a P.I. digging into my past," the doctor explained. "He's probably hacked into my computer files. Someone did, anyway."

"Is there a point to all of this?" Garrett challenged. "Are you saying you have something in those files you want to keep hidden?"

"I'm saying I don't like my privacy being violated. I participated in some private adoptions, along with my attorney, Irving Kent. Neither Mr. Kent nor I had anything to do with stolen babies and illegal adoptions."

Garrett didn't buy it. "Three and a half weeks ago, a woman named Lexie Rayburn delivered a baby girl. You were the attending physician. Afterward, you tried to kill Ms. Rayburn with an overdose of narcotics."

"No! I most certainly didn't."

"Then I welcome your explanation. Oh, and it better be a good one. Because then you're going to tell me where that baby is."

"I was the doctor at a delivery three and a half weeks ago, but I didn't try to kill the mother. I simply gave her a sedative because she became extremely agitated."

"Mothers tend to do that when their babies are stolen."

"The child wasn't stolen. It was a surrogate baby, and the surrogate father came and picked up the child."

Lexie huffed. "I'm Lexie Rayburn. Where did this so-called surrogate father take the baby?"

If Darnell was alarmed that Lexie was listening, he gave no indication. "I don't know."

"I don't believe you."

"But it's the truth." Darnell sounded beyond desperate now. "I need your help, Sergeant O'Malley. I don't know what's going on, but the reason I hired a bodyguard is because I think someone's trying to kill me."

"Welcome to the club," Garrett grumbled.

Darnell didn't have a response to that. "I want to meet with you. I want you to arrange for me to be protected."

"Oh, we're going to meet, all right, but first let me explain to you what kind of cop I am. I would have no qualms about putting a bullet in you if you harm the baby that you stole."

"I can't harm a child I don't have. I don't know where she is." And much to Garrett's surprise, he sounded honest. About that, anyway.

"Meet me in the courtyard of the Franciscan mission on Monte de Leon Street in one hour," Garrett ordered. "Come alone."

"You'll protect me?"

"You bet. But if you don't have some answers, the right answers, then you'd better start worrying about who's going to protect you from me."

"HAVE I MENTIONED THAT bringing you with me just wasn't a good idea?" Garrett asked. Again.

"Yes, you have," Lexie answered. "But we both know you didn't have a choice. Remember that part about not wanting to leave me at the safe house alone?"

"I should have waited for my brother to arrive so he could stay with you."

Lexie blew out a long breath. "Garrett, I can help you if something goes wrong. Not that it will," she quickly added when that look flashed through his eyes. The look of a man who wanted to strangle himself for going against his instincts. And his instincts obviously included keeping her hidden away while he took all the risk. "You arranged for an ideal meeting place."

Well, maybe not ideal. Nothing about this constituted ideal, but Garrett and she were in sort of a catbird seat. They'd arrived at the mission a good half hour before the meeting, and for most of that time they'd been waiting in the reception center that overlooked the courtyard. When Dr. Darnell showed up, they'd be able to see him, and they'd also know if he'd brought along any hired guns.

They didn't have the courtyard to themselves, which Garrett had likely anticipated. A few visitors were strolling the grounds and the buildings. There weren't enough people to call a crowd, but the lack of privacy hopefully meant that Darnell hadn't come to fight.

Garrett checked his watch. "Darnell should be here in five minutes."

"He'll show," Lexie assured him.

But before the last word had left her mouth, she heard a slight buzzing sound.

"My phone," Garrett said. He'd obviously set it on vibrate, probably so it wouldn't ring and alert anyone.

Lexie held her breath, praying that the doctor hadn't canceled.

"Anything he wants to say to her, he can say to me," Garrett responded to the caller.

Her heart sank. Darnell was likely canceling, and no doubt wanted to substitute a phone conversation for a face-to-face meeting. That couldn't happen. She needed to see how he reacted when they questioned him about the baby.

Garrett put his hand over the mouthpiece. "It's Billy Avery. Do you want to talk to him?"

All right. She hadn't anticipated that, and it took her a moment to shift gears. Yes, they needed to talk to Darnell, but they could perhaps learn something from Avery, as well.

Lexie cautiously took the phone. Garrett moved closer, until they were pressed up against each other in order to hear the conversation. But he also slipped his hand inside his jacket and put his hand on his gun. He didn't look at her. Instead, he kept his attention fastened on the courtyard.

"I'm getting calls and visits from cops, Lexie. Regarding a missing baby. Well, I just wanted you to know that I had nothing to do with it."

Although she didn't remember a lot about the time she'd worked for Billy Avery, Lexie hadn't expected him to make a confession, especially not over a cell phone.

"You know, you're the second person today who's said they didn't have any part in this," she informed him. "I'm getting tired of hearing it."

"But I'm telling the truth. And I'm also telling you to back off. If you don't, you'll be very sorry."

Beside her, she felt Garrett's arm tense as he checked to see whether or not Darnell had arrived. He hadn't.

"Let's clear up a few things," she said to Avery. "You know I'm not the bluffing type, and I will bury you if you've taken my child. You want to play? All right, here we go. Let's play. I'm within seconds of calling police headquarters and detailing every illegal thing you've ever done. Hear that, Billy? *Everything*."

"You know nothing."

"I know things about you that will make a prosecuting attorney salivate. Do you honestly believe I could work for a man like you and not know what you were doing? Think back—remember when you'd be talking on the phone to one of your cronies, and you'd wonder if someone was listening? Well, guess what? I was listening."

"You're bluffing."

"Am I?"

"I hope to hell you are bluffing, Lexie, because I'm not behind your baby's disappearance. If the cradle is empty, it's not because of me."

"I'm not convinced."

And with that, she hung up. She was about to explain to Garrett what she'd just done, then realized no explanation was necessary. He used his cell phone to speed dial a number.

"Brayden," he said a moment later. "Keep a close watch on Avery's calls and visitors. If he's behind this, he'll be contacting someone very soon."

"I was bluffing," Lexie admitted as soon as Garrett finished talking to his brother. "Other than what I provided during testimony at the trial, I don't have any other dirt on Billy Avery. Or if I do, I don't remember it."

"I figured. But threatening him like that was a good move. It might spur him to make a mistake." Obviously riled, though, Garrett glanced at her. "Of course, the mistake could be yours."

She readily nodded. "He might try to send someone after me, to make sure I won't tell the cops anything."

"Bingo. Man, when you annoy someone, you go for the number one scumbag in the state. At any time during your threats and bluffs did it occur to you that Avery might try to silence you permanently?"

"It occurred to me. But what would you have done in my place?"

He hesitated a moment. Cursed softly. "The same thing. Except I would have threatened to bash his face in."

"I considered that." And she was only partly joking. "I just hope what I did gets us some results."

"Oh, if Avery calls anyone, we'll know about it. And we'll follow visitors to see if they can lead us to the baby."

It was a good backup plan in case Dr. Darnell turned out not to be in a confessing kind of mood. Of course, it was entirely possible that Darnell was working for Avery.

If that was true, why would Avery want her dead? If the baby was his insurance policy, then he had all he needed to keep her silent. Or better yet, why hadn't he just had her killed the night she delivered? That would have ensured she never testified against him. Something didn't add up, especially since her former boss hadn't been surprised to hear from her after all this time. Or maybe it did add up, and she just hadn't made the right connection.

Remembering that they had yet another confrontation to face, she glanced around. "Still no sign of Darnell?"

"Not yet. But then, I figured he wouldn't be standing in the open. Especially if he has a boss who'd rather he not reveal anything about the illegal adoption…."

She followed Garrett's gaze, to see what had diverted his attention, and Lexie spotted the man. Not Dr. Darnell. This guy was older, probably mid-fifties, and he wore an expensive Italian suit. He crossed the courtyard and made a beeline toward them.

The man wasn't alone.

Dr. Linnay Blake, the Brighton Birthing Center director, was with him.

Garrett checked to make sure they had the reception center to themselves. At the moment, they did. And he drew his weapon just in case Linnay Blake and her friend were there to cause trouble. "Get back into that corner," he ordered Lexie.

That earned him a huff, and she nearly gave him a lecture about equal rights and such. But he obviously had enough on his mind. Lexie stepped back, deep into the corner, taking her own handgun from her shoulder purse.

The man opened the door, and Garrett took aim.

"Sergeant O'Malley?" the newcomer asked. He turned his cool hazel eyes on her. "Lexie Rayburn?"

"Who are you?" Garrett demanded.

"Well, I'm not someone who warrants being held at gunpoint."

Garrett kept his gun and his glare aimed at the man. "I'll decide that if you don't mind."

The glare must have worked at least a little because the man dropped back a step. "I'm Dr. Darnell's attorney, Irving Kent. And I believe you know Dr. Linnay Blake."

"They know me," Dr. Blake said coolly. "They lied their way into my clinic."

"We had a reason to lie," Lexie interjected.

"That may be, but that's not why we're here." Kent retraced that step and moved closer to them. He lowered his voice practically to a whisper. "Dr. Darnell called me about a half hour ago, said he had a meeting with you and Ms. Rayburn, and he asked me to come."

"He did the same to me," Dr. Blake explained. "He requested that I meet him here."

"Why would he do that?" Garrett asked.

Kent shrugged as if the answer were obvious. "He said it's because he didn't trust you, and he wanted me here, just in case." He glanced around. "I'm afraid *just in case* might have happened."

Kent's comment brought Lexie out of the corner. "What's that supposed to mean?"

Linnay Blake jumped in to answer. "It means Andrew Darnell was afraid of someone, and that someone might have intimidated him into skipping this meeting. You're wasting your time. Darnell's not going to risk his life for anyone or anything."

Irving Kent reached into his pocket. Not the best idea he'd ever had, and the startled look in his eyes proved that when Garrett pointed his gun right at his head.

"It's a business card," Kent explained. He extracted it from his pocket and held it out.

Garrett reached forward cautiously, and took it. "What am I supposed to do with this?"

"If Darnell shows, call me. I want him to explain why he wasted my time with this bogus appointment. Oh, and tell him I'll bill him double for it."

Kent didn't wait for Garrett's assurance that he would call. The attorney turned and walked away.

"So, why did Dr. Darnell want you here?" Lexie asked Dr. Blake.

She shook her head. "I have no idea."

"Really? You don't think it has something to do with the illegal adoptions?"

"Maybe. Maybe he wanted to bare his soul and wanted witnesses. Who knows? I meant what I said—Darnell is spineless. He'll never accept the blame for anything he's done wrong." She checked her watch. "And if you don't mind, I'm late for an appointment."

Lexie nudged Garrett's arm when Linnay Blake walked out. "Do we just let them go?"

With his jaw muscles twitching, he stared at the door. "I've got no reason to hold them. Yet. Besides, the person we need to speak to is Darnell. If either of them is guilty of anything, Darnell might be ready to tell us."

Lexie hurried to the doorway, but all she got was a glimpse of Dr. Blake disappearing down one of the shrub-lined paths.

"Darnell's not coming, is he?" Lexie groaned and smacked her hand against the wall. "This could have all been a setup."

"Trust me, I've considered that. That's why I didn't want you here."

She dismissed what he said with a shake of her head. "But if it's a setup, then why hasn't he already made his move?"

That's when they heard a woman scream.

"Stay here," Garrett ordered. And he would have rushed out the door if Lexie hadn't caught his arm.

"Alone?" she questioned. She didn't mind being

alone. In fact, she hoped like the devil that she had a chance to run into Darnell, but she didn't want Garrett going out there without backup.

There was another scream, followed by a shout for help.

Garrett fired a glance at Lexie and then in the direction of the scream, obviously debating what he should do. "Stay behind me, and don't try anything dangerous."

They made their way out of the reception center. Garrett stayed low, practically in a crouch, and Lexie positioned herself the same way. All the screaming and shouting was coming from a small group of people who had gathered at the far end of the courtyard.

"Police, nobody move," Garrett shouted out as they approached the group.

No one appeared armed, and none of the five people seemed to be on the verge of attacking. Instead, one of the terrified-looking women stepped aside and pointed to a thick row of sage bushes and Mexican heather. Huge oaks towered over the shrubs, making that particular section dark and a little eerie.

It got a lot eerier.

Because the woman pointed to a figure lying on the ground. A man crumpled in a heap, facedown.

And there was blood.

He'd been stabbed in the chest, and the bright red

stain had spread across the front of his crisp white dress shirt.

But even with the blood and the awkward position of the body, Lexie had no trouble recognizing him.

Dr. Andrew Darnell was dead.

Chapter Fifteen

The dream caused Garrett to wake up, and not peacefully. His eyes opened with a jolt that he felt throughout his body. It was a dream of bullets and death and failure.

His failure.

He hadn't been able to stop anything, including Lexie being hurt.

He snapped his head toward her and found her sleeping beside him. She had no injuries like the ones in his dream. She was safe.

For now.

Because although it had only been a dream, Garrett knew that in reality, Lexie could have been hurt when they'd been waiting for Dr. Darnell. It could have been her lying dead on the ground. He wanted to promise himself that she wouldn't be in harm's way again, but it was a promise he couldn't make. Or keep. Lexie and he were in this together, danger and all, and he couldn't exclude her any more than she could exclude him.

He checked the clock on the nightstand. It was nearly 6:00 a.m. Being in bed at that hour hardly constituted sleeping in, but it was for them, considering the enormous task ahead of them. Still, Lexie and he needed sleep. They'd been functioning on pure adrenaline and willpower for way too long. A tired mind certainly wasn't going to help either of them.

So, exhausted from the police interrogation and Darnell's murder, they'd collapsed into the bed at the safe house around midnight. Both were still wearing their street clothes. They hadn't taken the time for pj's, and because exhaustion had cooled the passion, he hadn't slept on the sofa after all. It was simply too much of an effort to locate bedding.

Lexie made a sound, a soft moan, drawing Garrett's attention to her. And she reached out. For what, exactly, he didn't know. But he made himself available. Knowing it was a mistake and not caring, he pulled her into his arms.

"Garrett," she whispered, her voice warm with sleep.

She lifted her arms, first one and then the other, and slid them around his neck. She leaned in and kissed him. He kissed her, too.

Yeah, that was another mistake. So was the way he deepened the kiss with his tongue when she responded with one of those breathy moans that rumbled low in her throat. The moan continued until she pulled back.

"I'm sorry." She groaned and dropped her head onto his shoulder. "I got caught up in my dream."

Well, he'd gotten caught up in the aftermath. "It must have been some dream."

"It was about you."

And judging from the sultry way she said it, her dream hadn't been about bullets and dying. "That's not a good thing to say to a man in your bed."

She looked him straight in the eye. "It wasn't adrenaline sex."

Garrett was having a little trouble following this conversation. "What wasn't? In the dream?"

"No. On the coffee table. I remember the attraction before that." She paused. Smiled. Grimaced. "I keep reminding myself that your lieutenant will punish you if you get involved with me again."

That was true. But there was another truth. "We're already involved."

She nodded. "Because of our child."

Maybe that was it. Lexie's bottom line for their involvement. Maybe it was his bottom line, too. Maybe their child and passion were all there was for her.

"Still, the dream was…hot," she added.

Garrett didn't intend to question her about it. Though judging from the slight smile that lifted the corner of her mouth, Lexie couldn't get it off her mind. Then the smile faded.

"Do you ever just want to forget, if only for a few minutes?" she asked. "Just for an instant, do you want to pretend that everything is all right? That our baby is over there in that bassinet?"

He wasn't sure where she was going with this, until she whispered, "I just want to forget for a few minutes, okay? I want to get lost in that dream with you."

And she kissed him again.

Garrett thought about resisting. He even tried. But she was right. Their kiss could make things feel better, if only for a short while. It was a much needed reprieve. With a high price, of course. However, at the moment all Garrett could think of was that she tasted even better than she looked, and that she was the best reprieve he'd ever been given.

Then things just spiraled out of control. It was as if a big neon sign were flashing in his head: Kiss Her, Kiss Her, Kiss Her.

So he did.

He placed one hand on her chin and slid the other around the back of her neck. He snapped her to him. Against him. Pressing hard. He kissed her as if she were the breath he needed in order to stay alive. As if this would be the last kiss either of them would ever experience.

She did her part. While his mouth devoured hers, she tightened the grip she had on him. He tightened his as well. He took and tasted and savored her, until he knew that kissing wasn't going to be enough. It only fueled the heat.

Touching made it worse.

Lexie started it, placing her hand on his chest. Specifically, her fingers circled his right nipple. It

really didn't matter what part of him she clutched—
he was one big erogenous zone.

Garrett released her chin so he could slide his
hand between their bodies and touch her breast. She
made a sound of pleasure and attacked his mouth.

Unfortunately, that deep, hot contact, coupled
with the touching, caused another neon sign to start
flashing in his head, a warning. Lexie might want
sex, but she might not be physically ready for it.

Plus, he didn't have a condom.

"What's wrong?" she asked as his hand froze. So
did the rest of his body.

"We can't have unprotected sex," he said with
some difficulty. "And I don't have a condom."

She groaned, cursed, groaned again, and buried
her face against his neck. Not good. It was a highly
sensitive area for him, especially with her warm
breath fanning his skin.

"Mercy. I don't think I've ever wanted something
this much. *You*," she corrected. "I want you, and no
amount of denying it will help. This wasn't a diversion. This was acting out a fantasy."

Oh, man. This was torture. Pure torture. And he
knew it couldn't get any better. Well, not for him,
anyway. But he could sure do something about Lexie.

Garrett turned, shifting her as well so that her
back was against the headboard. She reached for
him, in the right place. Or rather, the wrong place.
She reached to pull his body against hers.

He kissed her and gathered up her hands. "We can't do *that,* but I can take the edge off."

She stared at him a moment. "I can take the edge off for you, too," she offered.

Oh, that was tempting. "Better not. One of us needs to stay sane."

"I can stay sane." Since her eyes were already unfocused, he knew that wasn't true.

"No. You can't." Well, she wouldn't if he did this right. And Garrett intended to do it right. They'd been dancing around this for days. Heck, since the moment they'd met. Maybe it was the fatigue or the spent adrenaline, but he didn't want to dance around it this morning.

"Besides," he said, to remind himself more than to remind her. "You might not be ready for sex."

"I'm ready."

And to prove her point, she angled her hips so that her sex touched his. His eyes crossed. Since he couldn't possibly stay sane with her doing that, he eased back and occupied her mind with something else.

He unbuttoned her shirt, dipped his head down and kissed her cleavage. She was small. Firm. Perfect. And she responded by trying to make his eyes cross again. Garrett dodged her touch and did some touching of his own. He didn't stop the kisses on her breasts as he unzipped her jeans and slid his right hand across her stomach.

Then lower.

Past the waist of her jeans and into her panties. Such as they were. A swatch of silky fabric.

He touched her, easing his fingers over her skin. Lower. Easing his fingers inside her. She made a sound—the most erotic sound he'd ever heard. And he wanted to hear it again, so he continued touching her. Stroking her. Until Lexie was moving in rhythm against his fingers.

"You, too," she said, groping for his zipper again.

He stopped her by pressing his hand over hers. She added some pressure that made him question if he'd really be able to do this without turning it into full-blown sex.

But Garrett knew he could.

This was the right thing to do.

It helped that Lexie stopped struggling when he increased the strokes with his fingers. He stayed gentle. Well, as gentle as she would allow. She added pressure, increased the friction by pushing against him.

Her scent surrounded him. He took her mouth, wanting to feel and taste her. She was close. So close. Her body trembling. Her breath gusting. Her hips moving at a pace as old as time.

He felt her shiver against his fingers. He deepened the kiss. Deepened the pressure. He slid his body between her thighs, and she wrapped her legs around him. Pushing. Pressing. Taking.

"Yes," she said.

And she shattered.

She latched on to him, taking everything he was giving her. Everything. The tension left her body, and she collapsed against him.

"Give me a second," she mumbled through the rough gusts of breath.

"For what?" Garrett was doing some heavy breathing of his own.

Lexie moistened her lips, kissed him. "I can take the edge off for you, too."

He didn't doubt that. In fact, as locked and loaded as he was, one touch should do it. But they weren't going there. Because he didn't think this taking-the-edge-off stuff would last long. If he got naked, and if Lexie started touching him, he wasn't sure he had enough willpower to resist her.

Garrett kissed her gently. And not as foreplay.

Lexie obviously had no trouble interpreting that kiss. "This isn't fair to you."

"It is fair. Trust me, I had fun."

"Not as much as I did," she grumbled.

Since he was still in major discomfort and was testing the strength of the fabric of his boxers and his jeans, he didn't smile right away. But Lexie's smile coaxed his to life.

"I owe you," she said. And she went back for another round of kissing. Real kissing. With her tongue.

The doorbell rang. The sound shot through him, and for a second, he felt like a kid who'd just been caught stealing cookies. Not exactly a bad metaphor.

That guilty-pleasure feeling was quickly replaced by another. This could be a visit by someone who had information about the baby.

Or it could be someone who wanted them dead.

On his feet in an instant, Garrett grabbed his shoulder holster and hurried to the door. He looked out the peephole and spotted a man outside. Garrett recognized him. It was a fellow cop.

"I have something for you," the officer stated when Garrett opened the door. He handed Garrett two huge cardboard boxes stacked one on top of the other. Both were stuffed with manila folders.

"The P.I. you hired managed to locate these. We copied a set for the lead investigator and for Lieutenant O'Malley, but we thought it'd go faster if you went through them as well. Your brother said to remind you that we can't use the files to charge anyone with anything. Not officially, anyway. But you might be able to get some leads."

Garrett glanced at the files, and when he realized what they held, he thanked the officer and practically slammed the door in his face.

Garrett looked over his shoulder. He knew Lexie would be there, and she was.

"What is it?" she asked, her palm flattened over her heart.

"Dr. Darnell's adoption records."

Garrett didn't have to add that their daughter's file was likely in his hands.

LEXIE DIDN'T DARE get her hopes up, but it was impossible to ignore the fact that this might be the miracle they'd been looking for.

Garrett deposited the boxes on the coffee table. Neither of them wasted any time. She grabbed some files; he did the same.

After thumbing through several, Lexie learned that some contained scanned photos of the babies. Others were filled with handwritten notes of delivery times and adoptive parent info. They also contained the names of the birth mothers, but she figured those were likely to be bogus. After all, Darnell wouldn't have wanted a way for the mothers to prove that he'd stolen their children.

"There are dozens," Garrett mumbled. "And there are probably a lot more than this. God, how many lives did this man ruin?"

"Too many."

Theirs included. Because even when they found their child—and they would—they couldn't get back those weeks they'd lost. And Lexie would never forget the trauma this man had caused them. *Never.* It was too bad he was dead. She would have preferred him to be rotting in a jail cell. Besides, if he'd been alive, they possibly could have gotten the info from him.

The first four files were for infant boys, so she put those aside and continued going through the stack. The next was a girl, but she'd been born nearly three months earlier. Still, Darnell could have doctored the dates, so Lexie took a closer look. The baby looked like any other newborn, and Lexie didn't recognize anything distinctive. Not that she would. After all, she'd never seen her daughter's face.

Garrett and she continued the hunt. Sitting side by side on the sofa, each took a folder, thumbed through and then put it aside when the facts didn't match. With each file she discarded, Lexie could feel her hopes fading.

Until she got to the sixteenth folder.

There was a photo and sketchy details, and though some of those details weren't a precise match, it was the first one that seemed a real possibility.

"This could be her," Lexie said after she cleared her throat. "Though the dates don't match."

She passed the folder to Garrett, or rather tried to, but he didn't take it. Instead, he stared at it a moment, stood and yanked his wallet from his pocket. Almost frantically, he thumbed through some old photos, then held one out for her to see. It was a picture of two boys, one about six years old, the other about four. In the older boy's arms was a newborn—obviously, a girl, since she was wrapped in a pink blanket.

Garrett placed the photo on the table. "The baby is my sister, Katelyn." He placed the open file next to it and pointed to the picture of the adopted baby. "That's our daughter."

Lexie's heart began to race out of control. The rush of blood didn't help her breathing, and she suddenly felt light-headed. She picked up both the photo and the file and compared them.

There was a strong resemblance.

Too strong for it to be a coincidence.

She flipped through the pages in the file. There wasn't much. "Baby Dearman" had been born June 1st. The actual date Lexie had given birth was June 15th, but it was close enough. The child had weighed seven pounds, one ounce and was twenty inches long. Lexie had no idea if that information was correct.

"She's in perfect health," Garrett said, pointing to the doctor's notes. "No birth defects."

Lexie and he each gave a hearty sigh of relief.

The birth mother was listed as Alice Dearman, but other than the bogus name, the age and physical description fit Lexie to a tee.

"This is our child."

Garrett pulled Lexie into his arms for a celebratory hug. It only lasted a few seconds because both of them were anxious to see what else was in that file.

"The blood type matches mine," Garrett informed her. "We even have her footprint here so we can make a positive ID. We won't have to wait for DNA tests to make sure we have the right baby."

She could feel the excitement emanating from him, but her own chilled when they reached the last page. Lexie scanned through it twice, to make sure.

It felt as if someone were squeezing a fist around her heart.

Baby Dearman had already been scheduled for adoption. Her soon-to-be adoptive parents were identified only with the initials S.R. and M.R.

"Hell." Garrett swore.

And Lexie swore right along with him.

Because the adoption was scheduled for the following day.

A mere twenty-four hours from now, their baby would be handed over to a new family. If they didn't stop it.

That wasn't the worst part.

S.R. and M.R. were U.S. citizens, but they were abroad. They lived in an unspecified city in Egypt. Where the child would be flown.

Sweet heaven. If she went, it might take years of diplomatic red tape to get her back.

If ever.

That *if ever* chilled Lexie to the bone. It might already be too late. Her child could already be on a plane headed to the Middle East.

"Look." Garrett tapped the bottom of the page, drawing her attention there.

The man who'd authorized the adoption was none other than Darnell's attorney, Irving Kent.

"We're going after him," Garrett said. "Now."

Chapter Sixteen

Garrett hit the brakes of their rental car in front of Irving Kent's restored Victorian house. The attorney was home. Or he had been just five minutes earlier. They'd used their old ploy. Pretending to be a telemarketer, Lexie had phoned the residence, and Kent had answered.

"Now what?" she asked.

Sitting in the seat beside him, she was well past being tense. She was armed, ready and riled. Garrett wasn't sure he'd be able to hold her back. Heck, he wasn't sure he could hold himself back. The man responsible for their little girl's disappearance was in that house.

On the twenty-minute drive to the upscale Alamo Heights neighborhood, Garrett had considered calling his brother and asking for help, but he'd decided that might only complicate things. Even Brayden wouldn't be able to get a search warrant because the evidence was tainted. Darnell's adoption files had been illegally obtained and were therefore inadmissible in court, making them worthless for getting a warrant.

But those files had led them to the one person who could and *would* help them.

One way or another.

Garrett could almost feel the seconds ticking away, and he knew they didn't have time to waste. "Stay behind me," he said to Lexie as they got out of the car.

Of course, she fell in step beside him. "What are we going to do?"

Garrett huffed, pushed her behind him and glared at her so she'd stay at least partially protected. "I'm going to do what I do best."

It would cost him his badge. Maybe even earn him some serious jail time. He didn't care.

Garrett went onto the porch, drew back his size twelve Lucchese snakeskin boot and bashed it against the door. As expected, the wood splintered. He had that kick down pat. It only took a ram with his shoulder to bring the door off its hinges. When they'd slipped inside, he shoved it back in place so as not to alert the neighbors. Hopefully, no one was paying attention to the noise he'd already made.

Garrett heard footsteps and aimed his weapon at the man who came running down the stairs and into the foyer.

"What the hell are you doing here?" Irving Kent yelled.

Keeping a firm grip on his gun with one hand, Garrett seized Kent's shoulder with the other and slammed him against the wall, face-first. Paintings rattled. One fell, crashing onto the hardwood floor.

"Have you lost your mind?" Kent demanded, then used some vicious profanity to convey his anger.

"Pretty much. And if I were you, that'd concern me a lot." Garrett heard his own voice. Didn't recognize it. He was way too calm on the outside. Inside, there was a fierce storm brewing, and he intended to aim every bit of that dangerous energy at Irving Kent. "Because you see, I'm past the point of being desperate. And that means you're in very big trouble. Now, tell me where you're holding the Dearman baby."

Bunching up his forehead in a scowl, the lawyer tried to look over his shoulder, but Garrett held him firmly in place. "Who?"

Garrett nearly punched him, but then realized this slime had probably handled hundreds of these adoptions. He likely wouldn't remember one name. "The Dearman baby is an infant girl," Garrett explained. "She was born nearly four weeks ago at the Brighton Birthing Center."

Kent shook his head. "So? Do you think I care about some kid born there?"

Lexie nearly punched Kent. With her fist ready, she came flying across the foyer, and Garrett had to use his forearm to keep her from slugging the guy.

He didn't want Kent unconscious, and Lexie could incapacitate him.

Since this situation could obviously get even more out of hand, Garrett went for the direct approach. "The Dearman baby is our child. She was taken illegally right after Lexie gave birth, and I want to know where she is."

Kent glanced at him as if Garrett's ears were on backward. "I don't have that kind of information."

"For your sake, you'd better have it," Garrett warned through clenched teeth. "Let me refresh your memory. The child is scheduled to leave the country, probably sometime tonight or tomorrow."

And so he could look Kent right in the eye to gauge his reaction, Garrett spun him around, making sure he slammed the man's back against the wall. More pictures rattled. "If you don't tell me where she is, I'm going to start breaking your bones, one by one. It won't be pretty, and it'll hurt more than you can possibly imagine."

If that concerned Kent, he didn't show it. "You're a cop. You wouldn't do that."

"Oh, but I would." Garrett tossed his gun to Lexie so he'd have both hands free. He caught the collar of Kent's expensive suit and literally lifted him off the floor. "I'm not a do-gooder Boy Scout. I've got a mean, nasty edge that shows itself when someone I love is in danger. Guess what, I love my little girl, and you're the only thing standing in the way of my getting her back. Don't doubt this—I can and will break you, Kent."

To prove his point, Garrett bashed him into the wall. The lawyer said nothing. He was shaken up, but kept that defiant snarl on his mouth. So Garrett shoved him into the wall again, but this time put a forearm to Kent's throat.

"Where is she?" he demanded, adding pressure.

Kent swallowed hard and tried to maintain that badass expression, but Garrett was sure he could do badass better than the lawyer. "I want my daughter," he reiterated.

"Stop!" Kent gasped.

Garrett didn't let up. In fact, he added more pressure, his arm crushing Kent's throat.

"I didn't set up any of this. Darnell did," Kent confessed. "I just signed off on the papers. I had no idea Darnell was stealing the babies. I just figured he was buying off the mothers at the shelter and the home."

It was good information, if it was true, but it wasn't what Garrett wanted to hear. So when Kent didn't say anything more, he lifted his fist and aimed it at Kent's jaw. "Where. Is. My. Daughter?"

Oh, now there was fear, and it seemed as if he couldn't get out the explanation quickly enough. "If she's scheduled to be flown out within the next twenty-four hours, she's at a house near the airport. They won't take her out on a commercial airline. She'll be flown on a private jet through Canada and then to the Azores."

"What's the address of the house where they have her?" Lexie asked.

"It's 212 Skylark Lane."

Hearing the address kicked up Garrett's heart rate. And his hopes. "How many people are with her?"

"The nanny, of course. And probably at least two assistants."

"That's a nice word for armed guards." Garrett pulled back his arm and quickly searched Kent for any cell phone or communication device. He didn't find anything, so he shoved the lawyer into the foyer closet.

"If you're lying," Garrett told him, "I'll be back, and I'll hurt you so bad that you'll beg me to put you out of your misery. Understand?"

Kent nodded, his movements shaky and uncertain. "I didn't steal those babies."

"At this point, I don't care. But believe me, I will later." Garrett tied him up using Kent's own necktie and belt, trussing him like a turkey, and for good measure, Lexie and he shoved a marble umbrella stand and a heavy table in front of the door.

"You know where 212 Skylark Lane is?" Lexie asked as they hurried out the front door toward the car.

"I know the neighborhood," Garrett assured her. "We'll find it."

"Should we call your brother?"

"Not yet. Legally, his hands are tied. When we get

to the house, we'll look around. If the baby's there, then we'll call him."

Lexie waited a moment. A long agonizing moment. "And if she's not there—what then?"

"She'll be there," Garrett insisted. He couldn't believe otherwise. They were too close now.

They got in the car and sped away. It was just past morning rush hour, so there weren't a lot of cars on the suburban street. Maybe something would finally go their way.

Lexie drummed her fingers, then fidgeted. "That was some good bluffing back there—threatening to break his bones," she commented. "It worked." Maybe it was small talk, or maybe she just had to say something. Anything.

"I wasn't bluffing." It wasn't small talk for Garrett. He wasn't the bluffing type. "That's the kind of cop I am. The kind of man I'm capable of being."

She considered that a moment. Nodded. "Good. The situation didn't call for a negotiator back there. That door had to be bashed in, and real threats were the only thing Kent would have responded to." She kissed his cheek. "Now, let's get our daughter."

WHEN THEY SPOTTED the house at 212 Skylark Lane, a million things were going through Lexie's head, but the foremost thought was that her daughter might be inside.

Lexie might be within minutes of holding her.

Mercy. She'd begged and prayed for this, and it suddenly seemed within her grasp.

Unfortunately, the situation wasn't without risks. Huge ones. First, there could be any number of gunmen inside. If the situation got out of control, shots could be fired. Their baby could be in danger. Garrett and she would have to do everything within their power to make sure that didn't happen.

"Stay as quiet as you can," Garrett instructed. "I'd rather surprise them."

"I'd rather throttle them," Lexie whispered. She put her hand in her jacket pocket and curved her fingers around the gun, so she'd be ready.

"Let's hope throttling won't be necessary."

It was midmorning, but the sidewalks were clear. No joggers. No one walking a dog. It was a blessing. Their best bet was to sneak into the house undetected.

They crossed the side yard, staying behind a row of shrubs, and then went to the gate that led to the backyard. It was locked. That didn't stop them. Garrett climbed over and unlocked it from his side so she could enter.

He put his finger to his lips to caution her to silence, and they approached the nearest window. It was covered with plantation blinds, but Lexie could see through the sliver of space on the side that the room was dark and empty.

"Nothing," she relayed in a whisper to Garrett.

Crouching down, they moved across the porch to

a trio of windows. Garrett slipped ahead of her and flattened his back against the wall. He inched forward. So did Lexie. And then he stopped. She felt every muscle in his arm tense.

Lexie came up on tiptoe to look over his shoulder. Unlike the other room, this one was bright. There were fluffy white clouds and butterflies painted on the pale blue walls.

The room was also occupied.

There was a woman. Probably the nanny. She was tall, stocky. Formidable looking. But she wasn't nearly as formidable as the two men. Both were armed with shoulder holsters complete with semiautomatics. They were both frantically cramming things into a suitcase.

Baby things.

Clothes, bottles and even a little pink stuffed bear.

"Kent might have gotten loose and alerted them," Garrett whispered. "Or maybe this is just their scheduled time to leave."

Lexie heard him, but didn't really hear him. She had her attention focused on the baby.

Or rather the absence of a baby.

She could see a cradle in the center of the room— empty except for some pink bedding. Their daughter was nowhere in sight.

Lexie wanted to move to the next window to see if there was another bassinet or baby carrier, but the risk was too great. So she waited until the woman and the two gunmen left the room.

Then, frantically, she scanned the space, moving from one window to the next. Nothing.

"Get down," Garrett warned, and he dragged her out of view just as the trio returned.

Staying out of sight himself, he took out his phone and called for backup. Unfortunately, they wouldn't be able to wait for outside help. One of the men was closing the suitcase and hoisting it. He turned and walked out.

"He's probably going to the garage," Lexie said. "We can't let them get away."

"They won't."

The other man motioned for the woman to follow, and she reached down to retrieve something from the floor. It was a baby in an infant carrier.

Garrett and Lexie's baby.

Oh, heavens. Lexie had thought she was prepared for this moment, but she wasn't. Every part of her screamed to reach out and grab her child.

"I have to create a diversion," Garrett said. "I can't let them leave. We might lose them."

She nodded. She didn't like that "diversion" part, but knew they couldn't risk having those three people leave with their daughter. The airport was only minutes away.

"Don't do anything dangerous," she cautioned him, though both knew it was a useless warning. He would no doubt have to do something incredibly dangerous to get their child.

"You stay here. I'll try to keep the guards occupied until backup arrives."

With her heart in her throat, Lexie watched him disappear around the corner of the house. To put it mildly, she didn't have a good feeling about this, and part of her feared it would be the last time she would ever see him.

Because Garrett would die for them if necessary.

In some ways that was comforting, but it was mostly terrifying. She didn't want to lose him or their child.

She waited. Praying. Moments later, she heard the doorbell ring.

The doorbell!

She hoped Garrett wasn't about to launch into a gunfight with these men. No. He wouldn't do that. But he might try to win this battle with his fists. Not that she didn't trust his fists; she did. But he was outnumbered and outgunned.

The guard who remained in the kitchen said something to the nanny, and the woman carefully placed the carrier seat on the floor. The guard drew his weapon and made his way out of the room.

The doorbell rang again, followed by a heavy-handed knock.

The sound must have alerted the other guard, because he crossed back through the kitchen. No suitcase. He'd likely already put it in the car. But he was armed. He followed the other man toward the door.

Lexie debated what to do next, but the debate came to a quick halt when she saw the woman pick up the carrier. She and the baby were headed for the garage.

That was Lexie's cue to do something—fast.

Running, she went in the opposite direction from Garrett, made her way through the yard and to the side of the garage. Another gate. Locked. When she couldn't undo the latch, she climbed the fence and, as quietly as possible, dropped to the other side. She waited a moment to make sure the guards hadn't detected her, but they apparently hadn't.

There were voices—loud voices, shouts—all coming from the front. She saw Garrett sprint by, and moments later, both men in pursuit.

Lexie was terrified that he'd be shot, but the sound she heard was just as terrifying: the garage door opening.

Lexie broke into a sprint. Clutching her gun, she turned the corner to see the nanny putting the baby into the car seat. The woman was hurrying and didn't appear to be waiting for her comrades. She had keys in her hand.

She was obviously trying to leave with the baby.

"Stop!" Lexie cried.

The woman spun toward her, and that's when Lexie noticed the tiny silver handgun. A girl's gun, some people called it, but Lexie knew it was just as deadly as its higher caliber counterparts.

"That's my baby," she explained, nodding toward the child. "Dr. Darnell stole her from me."

If the woman had even a shred of sympathy, she didn't show it. "You'll have to work that out with Dr. Darnell."

"He's dead." And judging from the woman's expression, she knew that. "I'll work things out with you. Step away from the car."

The woman didn't hesitate, nor did she step away. Instead, she made the biggest mistake of her life. She aimed that little silver gun at the baby.

The fear hit Lexie first, raw and primal. But rage immediately followed. She was not going to let this woman hurt her daughter.

Lexie wasn't sure what happened. Something clicked in her head, memories flooded her brain and she charged at the woman. But she didn't tackle her. Instead, Lexie angled her body, kicked—higher than she could have imagined she could—and the little gun went flying out of the woman's hands. Lexie might have stopped there and reached for the baby if the nanny hadn't come at her.

Garrett had been right about her martial arts training. Lexie realized very quickly that she had the power to pound the woman into the floor. So that's what she did. She smashed the heel of her hand into the woman's chin, throwing her off balance. But Lexie wasn't taking any chances. She hooked her foot around the woman's knees and knocked her down.

Lexie glanced at the baby to make sure she was okay. The infant was sleeping peacefully in the car seat—unlike the nanny, who was now howling with pain. Lexie figured it wouldn't be long before her comrades came running to see what was wrong.

Trying to work fast, Lexie snatched up the car keys the woman had dropped on the ground. She used the keypad to open the trunk, and began dragging her toward it. Locking her in the trunk wasn't an ideal solution, because she could still yell for the guards, but it would keep her contained until backup arrived. And it would free Lexie to help Garrett with those two thugs.

The woman fought her and, in fact, tried to punch Lexie. Weary of the fight and anxious to get to her child, Lexie drew back her elbow and slugged her in the jaw. It worked. Well, sort of. Lexie had to do some pulling and tugging to get the now unconscious woman into the trunk. And she had to do that while keeping a grip on her gun in case the guards returned from Garrett's diversion. By the time she had the nanny inside and had slammed the trunk, Lexie was out of breath.

She forced herself to get moving, and fortunately, she had the ultimate motivation—her baby. Lexie scrambled toward the car, got in and started the engine. She reached back and touched her daughter's cheek. She couldn't help it. Though the baby didn't open her eyes, she lifted the corner of her mouth.

A smile.

Lexie felt that smile spread throughout her entire body. It was nothing short of a miracle.

She couldn't dwell on that miracle, though. There wasn't time. She needed to find Garrett and get out of there. They could use the car to get away, and maybe the backup officers could catch the guards.

But where was Garrett?

She was on the verge of backing out of the garage when she realized that probably wasn't a smart thing to do. If the gunmen saw her, they'd likely start shooting. That would put the baby in danger. First, she needed to find Garrett.

Lexie turned off the engine so there wouldn't be a buildup of carbon monoxide, and left the garage door open. With her gun gripped in both hands, she made her way back to the garage entrance. She listened first to make sure the nanny wasn't conscious and trying to get out of the trunk. All was quiet in that particular area. But not outside. She could hear footsteps.

Someone was running.

That sound was quickly followed by another.

A gunshot.

Lexie hadn't thought her heart could beat any faster, but she was obviously wrong. She wanted to call out to Garrett, but knew that could be a fatal mistake. It would draw the gunmen right to him, to her. And to the baby. Lexie had done some difficult things in her life, but staying put, not going after him, was one of the hardest.

She listened, trying to ignore the heavy pulse stabbing in her ears. No footsteps. No gunshot. But she did hear something.

A police siren.

The two thoughts hit her almost simultaneously. Their backup had arrived, but the sound of sirens might cause the gunmen to panic. They probably wouldn't want to leave witnesses—especially a cop.

Lexie tightened her grip and braced herself for whatever was about to happen.

She heard the footsteps again. Fast and furious, they were coming right at her. The sirens got louder as well, drowning them out, but she had no doubt that the runner was headed in her direction. She moved away from the car so that if there was gunfire, it would be aimed at her and not the vehicle.

"Don't shoot," she heard someone say.

It was Garrett.

She barely got a good look at him before he launched himself at her, dragging her to the floor. He didn't stay down with her, however. He came up on one knee, ready to fire.

"Where's the nanny?" he asked, not taking his attention from the garage entrance.

"In the trunk."

He gave a grunt of approval. "The officers are in pursuit of the gunmen. They probably aren't anywhere near here."

But Garrett obviously wasn't taking any chances.

Lexie released the breath that she hadn't even realized she'd been holding. It wasn't over, not by a long shot, but at least they weren't fighting this alone.

"Is the baby all right?" he asked.

"Yes. I think so."

He made an audible sound of relief. "There's an ambulance on the way. Just in case."

That was good. But Lexie could only think of one thing, now that she knew Garrett was okay. "She smiled at me."

He looked at her over his shoulder, and then his gaze drifted to the vehicle.

"I moved over here, away from the car," Lexie explained. "In case there were shots."

"Good thinking."

Lexie heard another siren. Definitely an ambulance.

"My memory returned," she told him.

He glanced at her again. "All of it?" he asked, obviously surprised.

"I think so." He probably had lots of questions. However, with that ambulance siren getting closer and closer, there was only time for her to answer the important ones. "I don't know anything that can be used to prosecute the people who took the baby. I didn't see or hear anything during the delivery that can help. But I do remember *us*."

The loud approaching siren cut off anything Garrett was about to say. The ambulance sped toward the house and came to a stop in the driveway. Two medics exited, and both of them raced toward her.

"Don't worry," Garrett assured her. "I know them. They aren't fakes."

Good. Because after the incident with the "cop" trying to run her off the road, Lexie didn't want strangers touching her baby.

The medics were rushing, and their sense of immediacy didn't do much to steady her nerves. Lexie felt as if she were being swept away in a surge of adrenaline and emotion.

"My baby," she managed to say. She pointed to the infant car seat. "I think she's okay."

One of the medics nodded. "We'll make sure."

That wasn't the hearty reassurance she'd been hoping for. Of course, a trip to the hospital was probably just a precaution, but considering everything they'd been through, even that was frightening.

Lexie and Garrett watched as the medic scooped the baby into his arms, put her in the ambulance and drove off. And the hollow feeling in Lexie's heart, the one that had disappeared the moment she touched her daughter, returned.

Chapter Seventeen

"The baby's going to be okay," Lexie assured him one more time.

But Garrett wasn't buying it.

For one thing, Lexie was pacing and fidgeting, exhibiting the same nervous behavior he was. Too bad all that nervous stuff was leading them nowhere. All they could do was watch while the doctor examined their baby.

She had to be all right.

Because there was no acceptable alternative.

Man, she was little. Her head fit right in the doctor's palm. She was too small to have had such a crummy start to life. Still, she looked well. Okay.

Actually, she looked amazing.

She had a dusting of reddish-brown hair and a round face. Garrett decided she was the most beautiful baby he'd ever seen, but he wasn't sure he could trust his opinion on this. Love seemed to play a huge part in his reaction, and there was no mistake about it—he loved this little girl.

His daughter.

He couldn't help but smile at the idea. He'd never planned for fatherhood, but he wouldn't go back and change what had happened. Not for anything.

"I have to draw blood now," the doctor informed them. "It'll be a little uncomfortable for her—a lot uncomfortable for you—so you might want to look away."

Not a chance. Garrett wasn't going to take his eyes off her. Lexie obviously felt the same, because she stayed put. But just in case Lexie got woozy, Garrett slipped his arm around her waist and pulled her to him.

With the doctor busy drawing blood from the baby, Garrett made a visual check for bruises or any other marks. Since she was wearing only a diaper, he was able to get a good look. There wasn't anything that he could see.

Thank God.

Because if he'd seen one, just one, he would have found Irving Kent and torn him limb from limb.

There was a tap at the door. It opened, and Brayden stuck his head inside. He glanced at the baby a moment and smiled before bringing his attention back to them. "Can I talk to you for a few seconds?"

Since he seemed to aim that question at both of them, they went into the hallway. But Garrett kept the door open so they could see the baby. Except he did have to look away when the blood was drawn. The baby whimpered. Kicked. Garrett mentally whimpered, kicked and agonized right along with her.

"We found Irving Kent right where you said he'd be—locked in the closet at his house," Brayden informed them. "We have him at headquarters. We're interrogating him, of course, but unless he confesses, I seriously doubt we can charge him with kidnapping."

That got Garrett's attention. "He knew where the baby was."

"Yes, and he'll claim he knew that, but that he had no idea the adoption wasn't legal."

This wasn't a surprise, but it was damn hard to hear. Garrett wanted someone to pay for what had happened to Lexie and their baby. He wanted that person to be Kent. Unfortunately, the evidence he'd used to find their daughter might not serve another purpose. Still, what a purpose it had served already.

"We've also brought in Dr. Linnay Blake and Alicia Peralta, the nurse from the Brighton Birthing Center who spoke to you about Dr. Darnell," Brayden continued. "They're at headquarters undergoing interrogation."

Even with all the stress, Garrett could appreciate how quickly his brother had sprung into action. "I want to question them," Garrett insisted.

"You can't. Personal involvement aside, you've been placed on administrative leave pending an investigation of your actions." Brayden paused, cursed softly. "Garrett, you could permanently lose your badge. For now, you'll just lose it temporarily."

He nearly told his brother where he could shove that badge, but it wouldn't be fair to Brayden, and it would be the anger talking. Oh, yeah. Garrett was angry. Furious, actually. But aiming that fury at his brother would only make things worse. He wanted to aim it at Irving Kent and those two gunmen.

Garrett knew the drill from witnessing other officers in hot water. He knew what had to be done. He unclipped his badge from the waistband of his jeans and removed his weapon from his shoulder holster. He handed both to Brayden. It was like losing a piece of himself. It also hurt to know that this had to disappoint his brother.

"I'm sorry," Lexie said. She touched his arm, rubbed gently.

Garrett was sorry, too. About the badge, but not about saving his baby. If he had to make that decision a million times, he wouldn't have changed what he'd done.

"You'll get this back," Brayden promised.

"What are Linnay Blake and Alicia Peralta saying in the interrogation?" Garrett asked. Best to focus on what needed to be done rather than what had just happened.

"They've all denied any wrongdoing. I can't blame them. We don't have any evidence we can use to charge them."

"What about what I personally witnessed?" Lexie asked. "Someone at Brighton stole our baby. Wouldn't that be enough to hold Dr. Blake and Nurse Peralta?"

"It's thin at best, and they both immediately lawyered up. I don't think we're going to get them to say much. It's the same for the two guards and the nanny. All have lawyers, and none are talking."

"So then what?" Lexie demanded, her voice barely under control. "You just let them all walk?"

"For now, we have to let Dr. Blake, Kent and Nurse Peralta go. We can hang on to the guards and the nanny awhile longer, but their lawyers are already claiming they had no idea the adoption was anything but legal."

"Then why did they try to run when they saw us?" Lexie asked.

"They said they fought back because they thought they were victims of a home invasion."

So there might be a charge against Lexie and him. That wasn't totally unexpected. The guards and the nanny would probably do anything to keep up the pretense of being innocent.

Brayden gave him a brotherly jab on the arm. "But we'll continue our investigation. And this time, we won't cut corners. Now that the baby is safe, we can go about this the right way, with warrants and surveillance. Whatever it takes. And if we can't nail them for what they did to you, then we'll see what else we can charge them with."

Garrett silently cursed. It wasn't enough. Not nearly enough. But he also knew that he'd had a major role in tainting that evidence.

There was some movement in the examining room. The doctor stood, draped a white hospital blanket around the baby and picked her up.

"Everything appears to be fine," he said, walking toward them. "You've got a healthy baby girl here. Eight pounds, thirteen ounces."

He handed her to Garrett, who was unprepared for something so monumental. He had a split second of panic that he'd drop her, but she settled right into his arms. No shrieks. No squirms. Her gray-blue eyes met his. She squinted a little, as if trying to focus, and it appeared she was studying him. The incredible moment lasted only a few seconds before her eyelids drifted down.

Garrett looked at Lexie. She, too, was a little panic-stricken. And totally in love with the baby. They shared a smile.

"You'll be glad to know that her footprint matches the one in the file," the doctor stated. Garrett had to force himself to pay attention. No easy task with the warm bundle snuggled against him, and with Lexie snuggled against his arm.

"Blood type?" Brayden questioned.

The doctor hitched his thumb toward Garrett. "The baby's blood type matches his."

"So she's definitely an O'Malley," Brayden

declared, looking at Lexie. "We O'Malleys have AB negative. It's very rare."

"I knew she was an O'Malley when I saw her picture," Garrett said.

Brayden nodded. "Yeah. She resembles her aunt Katelyn."

"Lexie's hair, though," Garrett commented.

Lexie joined the conversation. "Garrett's mouth."

The doctor cleared his throat, probably to get their attention off the baby musings. "I also collected DNA from Lexie, Garrett and the baby and performed a DNA test. I'll do a rush processing. A private lab should have the preliminary results for you late tomorrow." He turned to Brayden. "Unless you need the results for some criminal prosecution? If so, that'll take a lot longer."

"Do both," Brayden insisted. "And do everything by the book. No shortcuts."

"Wouldn't think of it. I'll run the blood work myself, but I don't anticipate any health problems. The baby was well cared for and well fed."

That was something at least, but it wouldn't dissolve all the fear and anger Garrett still had steaming inside him. Another few minutes and the nanny and guards might have had the baby out of the house and on the way to the airport. If that had happened, he certainly wouldn't be holding his little girl in his arms.

The doctor excused himself to take care of the

blood tests, and Brayden didn't say anything until the man was out of earshot.

"I don't want anyone to know this, but I want Lexie, you and the baby back at the safe house. With a police guard," Brayden added.

Garrett didn't need any clarification. If all their prime suspects walked, that meant one or more of those suspects might be gunning for them. After all, one had already murdered Darnell and tried to kill them.

Brayden checked his vibrating pager, and then his watch. "I'll arrange for diapers, formula and bottles to be delivered, but I want you three to stay put."

"We will," Lexie promised.

That apparently wasn't good enough, because Brayden turned to Garrett. "*You'll stay put,*" he repeated.

Garrett brushed a kiss across his daughter's forehead. "We'll stay put." He looked at his brother. "Thanks for everything."

Brayden brushed his finger over the baby's cheek. "You have a name for her yet?"

Garrett and Lexie exchanged glances. They shook their heads. "Not yet."

"Better do it soon before Mom and Dad start making *suggestions*. You could end up with some obscure Celtic name like Bodelia." He paused and made a sound to indicate he wasn't totally joking. "As soon as things settle down, they'll want to see her."

That was a given. The O'Malleys were a tight-knit

family, and they'd want to cuddle and spoil the latest addition. Too bad that family bonding would have to be delayed because there was a killer out there.

A uniformed officer rounded the corner and motioned to Brayden. "I'll be right back," Brayden told them, and he walked down the hall to meet with the man.

Lexie snuggled against Garrett's arm again. "We did it, Garrett. We got her."

Yeah. And he had to smile in spite of the uncertainties that lay ahead. Not just uncertainties about the investigation, either. There were personal things to work out. Like calm-headed interrogations, he kinda sucked when it came to that sort of thing. But he figured Lexie and he were looking at shared custody.

Well, until they could figure out where this whole attraction thing was taking them.

Of course, if the killer wasn't caught, they'd have to remain at the safe house indefinitely. Though Garrett wasn't looking forward to being excluded from the investigation, Lexie and he could use the time to work out the issues surrounding the baby.

Lexie pressed her own kiss to the child's forehead, and that's when Garrett realized he was being selfish. He leaned toward Lexie and deposited their daughter into her arms.

"You didn't hold her back in the garage, did you?" he asked.

"No. There wasn't time."

So this was Lexie's first physical contact with their baby. He watched her face. Man, she beamed. He totally understood how she felt, and he was able to get that same high sensation by watching her reaction.

"I'm scared," she whispered.

"So am I."

She frowned. "You're admitting that?"

"Seems silly not to. But don't worry—I'll protect her, Lexie."

"I never doubted it."

Somehow, her absolute confidence shook him. And pleased him.

"We're her parents," Lexie said, her voice an odd mix of pride, defiance and love. "We made her."

"On a coffee table." Which didn't really add to the moment. "But we'll keep that part to ourselves."

Because the situation seemed to call for it, he bent his head and touched his mouth to hers. Lexie gave a sigh—part relief, part satisfaction. She slid her free hand around the back of his neck, and probably would have returned the kiss if they hadn't heard Brayden approaching. They quickly stepped away from each other.

"We have some news," Brayden said, walking toward them.

Garrett shook off the effects of that kiss and tried

not to sound annoyed at the interruption. "It'd better be good."

"It has potential. The nanny wants to talk. In exchange for immunity from prosecution, she's ready to name her boss."

Chapter Eighteen

For Lexie, it was a strange feeling—holding her precious baby while Garrett and she were escorted into police headquarters. She wanted to get her daughter as far away from the suspects as possible. However, she and Garrett had to learn the truth. They couldn't get on with their lives until they'd solved the riddle of who wanted them dead.

"You don't have to do this," Garrett reiterated. "You can wait at the safe house with a police guard. That's what Brayden wants us to do anyway."

"I know he does. But I *have* to do this. After everything we've been through, I have to hear what the nanny has to say. If the woman gives names, then this could all end here." And if so, Lexie wanted to be there, to celebrate with Garrett.

Brayden led them down a corridor lined with offices and interrogation rooms. "You'll be able to watch through a one-way mirror. You won't be able to question her." He aimed that remark at Garrett, who responded with an acknowledging humph.

Brayden opened the door to the observation room, but before they could step inside, Lexie heard someone call out.

It was the nurse, Alicia Peralta.

Garrett positioned himself protectively in front of the baby and her, but Lexie didn't think such measures were warranted. For one thing, Alicia had no purse that she could use to carry a concealed weapon. Besides, she'd likely been frisked. But Lexie wasn't about to rule her out as a danger.

"Ms. Peralta," Brayden said in greeting. "You should be in the waiting room."

"I was. But I needed to use the ladies' room." Her gaze landed on the baby, and she stepped forward. Both Brayden and Garrett blocked her from going closer.

"Oh," she said, her face flushed. "I'm sorry. Of course you're concerned about safety. I don't blame you after everything you've been through."

Yes, and Lexie couldn't discount the possibility that this nurse might be behind the illegal adoptions. Except she had given them a vital piece of information that had ultimately led to the baby's rescue. "Thank you for telling us about Dr. Darnell."

"I wish I could have done more, but Dr. Darnell covered his tracks."

Not entirely. Lexie thought of the box of files at the safe house. The P.I. and his staff had been able to find them, and each file potentially represented a baby who'd been stolen.

"I want to warn you about Dr. Blake." Alicia lowered her voice to a whisper. She glanced over her shoulder. "Dr. Darnell must have had someone helping him, and I believe that person is Dr. Linnay Blake."

"You've told this to the investigating officer?" Garrett immediately asked.

The flush on her cheeks deepened. "No. My attorney says I should keep quiet."

"Reconsider that." Garrett made it sound like a demand rather than a request. "If you're truly innocent, then telling the truth will only exonerate you. And it'll put the guilty people out of commission so they can't steal anyone else's baby."

Alicia nodded, though she appeared uncertain. Lexie had no idea if the woman would pass on any information to the investigator or not. She also had no idea if the information would be the least bit useful. After all, the cops already suspected Dr. Blake, and the doctor had the means and opportunity. Motive, too, since the illegal adoptions were bringing in lots of cash.

"You'll want to return to the waiting room," Brayden advised the nurse. It wasn't really a suggestion. He turned and put his hand on Lexie's shoulder to get her moving into the observation room.

"You don't trust her?" Lexie asked.

"No." Brayden and Garrett answered in unison. It

was Garrett who continued. "She could have pointed the finger at Darnell and Linnay Blake only to throw suspicion off herself."

That was true. But Dr. Blake could have done the same. Of course, maybe both were innocent. Hopefully, the truth would soon come out.

Lexie held her sleeping daughter against her chest and stared at the officer and the woman in the interrogation room. Just seeing the nanny brought back a flurry of bad memories. And anger. After all, the woman had pointed a gun at the baby. Lexie would never forget, or forgive, that.

"The nanny's name is Belinda McAllister," Brayden murmured "The doctor examined her and has given her an all-clear to be interviewed." He pressed an intercom button on the wall and instructed the officer to proceed.

The preliminaries took a few moments—the officer recording the nanny saying that she was voluntarily giving this information so she would be considered a cooperative witness. The woman eagerly nodded after each sentence.

"Enough," she said. "Let's just get this done. The man I work for is Irving Kent."

"WE'VE ARRESTED KENT, the nanny and the guards," Brayden explained.

Garrett wasn't surprised about that. He knew his brother would come through for him. He turned on the speaker phone so he could continue to listen to Brayden while going through the bags of supplies that had been delivered to the safe house. It wasn't that what Brayden was saying wasn't important. It was. But Lexie was feeding the baby and was in need of a bib. Garrett was in need of a shirt. He'd finished his shower minutes earlier and had located clean jeans. But no boxers. And no shirt.

"Is Kent talking?" Garrett asked.

"He's denying any involvement."

That wasn't a surprise, either. Garrett hadn't expected a lawyer to start spilling his guts on the testimony of one witness. Not without some kind of deal on the table, and that wasn't going to happen. Brayden had already promised there'd be no deals for Irving Kent.

Garrett rummaged through another bag. "Do you happen to remember which bag the baby's bibs, my shirts and my underwear are in?"

"Not a clue," Brayden answered. "I asked Katelyn to pick up the stuff."

He wanted to groan. Katelyn was the one member of the O'Malley clan with a bent sense of humor. Heaven knew what she'd put in the bags. Garrett gave up all hope of finding boxers.

He went through another bag and nearly cheered when he located a bib, a little pink swatch of terry cloth with stitching that said Daddy's Little Diva. In fact, everything in the bag was pink.

Except for a package of condoms.

He didn't know whether to thank Katelyn or threaten to smother her. He might do both. Especially since he was going to be walking around without underwear and a clean shirt. Fortunately, his sister had done all right with Lexie.

Well, sort of.

Thanks to Katelyn, Lexie was wearing a loose, peach-colored cotton dress that hit just above her knee and managed to skim every curve of her body. She certainly didn't look as if she'd given birth merely a month earlier. Man, she had some legs. Long, lean.

And distracting.

"Back to Kent," Garrett snarled. He stuffed the condoms deeper into the bag and went back across the room to put the bib around the baby's neck. Lexie was on the bed, infant in her arms, and their daughter was doing a good job of draining her bottle while she made the occasional slurping sound. "Do you plan to interrogate Kent yourself?" he asked Brayden.

"No. I'll send in Katelyn. But even that might not work. Kent has friends in high places. It's my guess that he'll take the fifth and make bail before morning."

That was *not* what Garrett wanted to hear. Still, the safe house was, well, safe, and even if Lexie and he had to stay there for days, at least he was with the very people he wanted to be with. Wanted to protect.

"If Kent makes bail, we can keep a close watch

on him," Brayden explained. "But there isn't much we can do if he has hired guns. Kent doesn't know where the safe house is, so as long as you stay put, you should be okay." With that warning, Brayden said goodbye and hung up.

"This isn't over," Lexie mumbled.

No. It wasn't. In some ways, it'd just begun.

Still, that wasn't something Garrett wanted to dwell on. He'd done all he could to protect them. They were at a safe house with a police guard parked out front. Garrett was armed. Lexie's gun was nearby. And they'd locked every window, every door. It wasn't exactly a fortress, but it was the best they could do.

Lexie finished feeding the baby her bottle, and set it aside so she could put the infant on her shoulder and burp her.

"You look like you know what you're doing," he commented, observing the process. Burping shouldn't have been such an enthralling subject, but it certainly seemed to capture his attention.

Lexie flexed her eyebrows. "Not really. I'm just doing what I've heard other people say they do."

"Good thing, too. Babies barf if they're not burped."

As if on cue, their little girl delivered a rather impressive burp that had them both chuckling.

Man, they were so smitten.

And since when had he thought of words like *smitten?*

They were obviously in deep trouble, but trouble had never felt this good. This right.

Lexie eased off the bed and, evidently trying not to make a sound, deposited the baby in the nearby bassinet. It was waist-high, freestanding and draped in white eyelet lace. Very appropriate bedding for Daddy's Little Diva.

"We need a name," Garrett said softly. "Brayden was serious about that Bodelia stuff. My family's really big on suggestions. Not necessarily good suggestions, either."

Lexie turned, looked at him. "Is this your way of taking my mind off the fact that Irving Kent will soon be a free man?"

She knew him too well. "Yeah. Is it working?"

"No. But at least Kent has no idea where we are." She gave a weary sigh and sat back on the bed. "Any luck finding your underwear?"

And she said it with a straight face, too.

"No, because I'm sure Katelyn didn't pack any. No shirt, either. But she did include an enormous box of condoms."

He waited for Lexie to laugh or make some witty comment about that. But she didn't. She just moistened her lips and then checked to make sure the baby was asleep. She was.

"What are you thinking?" Garrett asked. But he wasn't really looking for an answer. That sexy peach dress, Lexie's hot legs, a sleeping baby and condoms.

Those things, coupled with the look in Lexie's eyes, were the best answers.

She reached out, touched her fingers to his chest. "I can take the edge off," she offered, repeating what he'd said to her the night before.

They shared a smile.

"I can do better than that," he promised.

That drew some battle lines. And it was a battle. Or rather, it was about to be.

Lexie reached for him.

He reached for her.

They grappled for position and each other, and somehow landed on the bed and not the floor. They were starved. Desperate. But Garrett wasn't so crazed that he didn't realize his desperation, his need, was only for Lexie.

He kissed her the way he wanted to kiss her. She tasted like everything he'd ever wanted but always been denied. Like something forbidden. Yet welcoming.

"Should we be doing this?" he asked.

"Yes." And she said it without a shred of hesitation.

Good. Because he didn't want to stop.

Obviously, neither did she. She rolled them over and landed on top. Straddling him. The soft mattress created something of a tunnel, cocooning them in the only place they wanted to be.

With his help, her dress came off, and they sent it flying. It was the same for her bra and panties. Though Garrett had no idea why they were rushing, for some reason, speed counted. Of course, desperation could do that to two people who were about to explode if they couldn't have each other. They'd waited so long for this.

"No use of hands this time," Lexie warned, reaching for his zipper.

Since that seemed a little like a challenge, Garrett didn't use his hands. Lexie was there, naked, those long legs straddling him. So he adjusted his weight, flipped her over, made his way down her body and used his mouth instead of his hands. He slipped his tongue into the warm, welcoming heat of her body.

She gasped, moaned, melted and grabbed him by the hair. Though she did manage to say, "No fair."

Garrett didn't let up. He was enjoying himself too much, and knew for a fact that Lexie was, too.

And then everything got even crazier.

She hooked her legs under his arms and flipped him over, breaking the intimate contact. That didn't last long. She backed him against the headboard. Actually, she body slammed him, and with the expression of a warrior, went after his zipper again.

"We're doing this together, understand?" she asked.

Garrett knew it wasn't really a question when she downed his zipper and took him into her hand. She wasn't gentle. But then, he wasn't exactly in the mood for gentle. With her, though, that was another thing. He would be gentle, since this was her first time since giving birth, but Lexie let him know that she intended to show him no such consideration.

With that in mind, they tortured each other. There was no other word for it. Erotic torture. With her hand moving roughly over him. With her naked body pressed hard against him. Their mouths devouring each other.

The tension built.

The lust skyrocketed out of control.

And Garrett knew they had to do something.

"A condom," she said, scrambling off him and the bed to rummage through the bags.

He almost got up and helped her. But he rather enjoyed the view of a frantic, naked Lexie tossing clothes and other items from the bag. Plus he needed the momentary reprieve. He figured he was going to need every ounce of willpower and stamina to make this more than a quickie. He didn't mind quickies. But he wanted this to be memorable for Lexie.

It was already memorable for him.

Because he knew he would take her. On this bed. Right here, right now. He would fill her, sweep her to the edge. And over it. But it wouldn't stop the desperate need he had for her. It would only serve as a reminder that no other woman could take her place.

"Got it," she announced.

She tore at the wrapper as she made her way back to him. However, when she got to his legs she stopped and looked at him. "Those jeans are coming off—now."

LEXIE TRIED TO BE QUIET because she was well aware that her infant daughter lay sleeping on the other side of the room. Lexie was also aware that she was finally about to do something she'd wanted to for days—have her way with Garrett O'Malley.

Of course, the downside was that he would have his way with her. Except that wasn't really a downside. She'd already been on the receiving end of his edge-soothing ways, and she wanted more.

She wanted *all* of him.

Lexie fought with his jeans. It was worth the struggle when she got him naked. Part of her, the lust-crazed part, wanted to jump him here and now. No preliminaries. Definitely no wait. But she took a moment to savor the view.

Simply put, he was hot.

He was hot in jeans and a shirt. And he was especially hot naked and aroused.

Their eyes met, and despite the firestorm inside them, she made her way back up his body so he could kiss her. He was good at that, too. Aggressive but not smothering. He made her feel as if she was the most desirable woman on earth.

The slow, burning kiss fueled the fire. Too much. And Lexie found herself hurrying again to get the condom out of its wrapper.

Garrett slowed her hands a little by helping, but she made certain that she tortured him when she put on the condom. Of course, his torture soon became hers. After all, she was straddling a hot, aroused man whom she wanted more than her next breath.

So Lexie took him.

An inch at a time. Testing her own body. And realizing that the fit was a little tighter than she'd expected. It was also better, and that was saying something, because she'd expected the best.

"Are you okay?" Garrett asked, pausing. Probably so he could make sure she wasn't uncomfortable.

She wasn't—not from the fit, anyway, but from the unfulfilled need already clawing inside her.

Lexie moved, taking him farther into her body. Sliding against him. Urging him deeper.

Garrett added his spin to things. He grasped her hips, guiding her, creating the rhythm that both of them needed.

Mercy, did they need it.

So she let the need drive her. She moved faster, sliding against that hard heat.

Taking.

Giving.

Until neither could take or give any more.

She moved against him one last time. It worked. He arched his hips and gave her exactly what she was looking for—Garrett.

IT TOOK LEXIE several minutes to come back to reality. She listened for sounds in the room, but the only thing she heard was Garrett's and her rasping breaths. Thankfully, their baby had slept through the firestorm.

Lexie leaned forward, located his mouth and kissed him. "You're better in bed than you are on a coffee table. I didn't think that was possible."

"*We're* better in bed," he corrected. "Unfortunately, if you're interested in an immediate round two, I don't think I can move."

"Then don't. Round two can wait, and we can stay naked." Because Lexie feared she was temporarily paralyzed from the exertion.

"You say that now, but you'll want to be clothed when the baby wakes up."

Lexie grumbled in agreement, because he was right. And they forced themselves to get off the bed and dress.

"I'm glad my out-of-shape body didn't disgust you," she commented when she noticed the tummy bulge that rested on the top of her panties. Obviously, one of the side effects of the pregnancy.

Though he was still dressing, he took a moment to look at her stomach. "You have a great body. A woman's body. A very desirable body." He hooked an arm around her, kissed her. "I'll let you in on a little secret—I haven't lusted after a sixteen-year-old girl's body since I was a sixteen-year-old guy. It's *your* body that I want."

Fully clothed, fully sated and fully exhausted, they got back in bed. And she soon learned that Garrett was a bona fide spooner. She smiled sleepily, pleased at the information. In fact, Lexie was pleased about a lot of things happening in her life.

Of course, there were two big question marks: catching the person responsible for the kidnapping, and figuring out how they could make this whole family issue work. Both were daunting.

Answers would have to wait until tomorrow.

Lexie couldn't stop her eyelids from drifting closed. She snuggled against Garrett, his scent and warmth surrounding her. Embracing her. She was about to surrender totally to the fatigue and sleep when she heard a sound.

Garrett must have heard the noise as well, because he snapped to a sitting position and reached for his gun. Lexie got her own gun, eased off the bed and hurried to the baby. She didn't pick her up for fear of waking her and having her cry. It was probably best to stay quiet until they knew what they were up against.

A terrifying thought.

They waited, the silence settling in around them. Until they heard the sound again.

Footsteps.

Someone was in the house.

Chapter Nineteen

Garrett hoped like the devil that their visitor was the police office assigned to guard them. Maybe the guy was in search of a midnight snack or something. But if so, he would no doubt have alerted them that he was coming inside.

So that meant Kent could have made bail and come after them. Or any of the suspects the police had released from custody.

Garrett hurried to the bedroom door and locked it. A simple lock wouldn't be much of a barrier for someone who truly wanted to get inside the room, he knew. Though the only illumination was the moonlight filtering through the blinds, he had no trouble seeing Lexie. She was there. Waiting. Her left hand flattened over her chest, her gun in her right hand.

He motioned for her to take the baby into the closet. Keeping the infant in the bassinet, she rolled it there. When it wouldn't fit, she pushed the bassinet behind the closed closet door and stood in front of their baby. Protecting her.

Garrett only hoped that kind of protection wouldn't be necessary.

The footsteps continued. Whispers, too. The sounds were coming from the hall outside their bedroom door now, and he could tell there was more than one person out there. His best guess was three. Maybe four.

That didn't do much to make him breathe easier.

Keeping his gun aimed at the door, he hurried to the nightstand and grabbed his communicator. He pressed the two-digit code for the officer out front. The man should have answered immediately.

He didn't.

Nor did he answer when Garrett tried again.

Hell.

It meant the officer was likely incapacitated or worse, and Lexie and Garrett were trapped inside with the intruders and no backup. He didn't even try the phone line, figuring it'd been cut. Instead, he used his cell phone to call for help.

He made brief eye contact with Lexie to try and reassure her that they'd be okay, but she knew what was happening. And the fear was all over her face. Not fear for them, but for their child. Even if Kent was after revenge and not the baby, that didn't mean their daughter couldn't be hurt in a shoot-out.

"O'Malley?" someone called from the other side of the door. Not Kent, though. Probably one of his hired guns. "Your guard isn't *available* to help you, and your cop buddies won't be here for at least fifteen to twenty minutes."

Garrett knew that was, unfortunately, true. Fifteen to twenty minutes was a lifetime. But somehow, some way, he had to keep Lexie and the baby safe until then. "What do you want?"

"Your cooperation. If you cooperate, your baby won't be hurt."

He heard Lexie suck in her breath. Thankfully, the infant didn't make a sound. Garrett prayed she'd stay asleep so she wouldn't witness any of this.

"What's your definition of cooperation?" he demanded.

There were whispers. Profanity. "I'm going to kick in the door. If you shoot, we'll shoot back, and we won't be careful with our aim."

So, in this case cooperation meant their attackers wanted him to stand there while they killed them.

That wasn't going to happen.

"I have a better idea," Garrett countered. But before he could continue, there was a loud crashing sound. Two of them, in fact. The door flew open and he came face-to-face with a pair of armed gunmen. Both carried semiautomatics rigged with silencers.

"Drop your weapons," the larger man suggested. "And remember that part about bullets flying. You wouldn't want your little girl to get hurt."

Though that comment chilled his blood, Garrett

pushed it aside so he could do some bargaining. "Let Lexie and the baby go. Then we'll work out whatever needs to be worked out between us."

"I'm afraid we can't do that. The baby will go to her new parents. My boss doesn't want to lose all that money. You and the birth mom—that's a different story."

Not really. It was a story Garrett had already anticipated. "You're going to try to kill us?"

"Bingo. Except I'm going to do more than *try.* I'm going to succeed."

With that, the man turned his gun toward Lexie and slid his index finger over the trigger.

Garrett didn't have time to think; he dived across the room. He heard the swoosh of sound from the silenced shot, like someone blowing out a candle. He returned fire, but it wasn't fast enough to stop what the other man had already put into motion.

And Garrett felt the hot bullet slice through him.

FOR LEXIE EVERYTHING seemed to move in slow motion. Yet it was fast, too. Like rapid images from her worst nightmare.

First there was the bullet fired through the silencer, and a split second later, Garrett's own shot. Not silenced. Deafening. The baby immediately started to cry, and Lexie sent her a quick glance to make sure she was okay. She was, but the sound had obviously frightened her.

It had terrified Lexie.

Garrett fell at her feet, and she saw the blood on his arm. She felt fear claw through her. And anger. Especially the anger. These goons had not only hurt Garrett, they'd put the baby in danger.

They could have killed Garrett.

And maybe they had.

Maybe he would die not knowing that she loved him. And she did love him. She knew that now. She only hoped it wasn't too late to tell him.

Lexie didn't think. Going on pure instinct and adrenaline, she dived away from the bassinet to draw fire away from the baby. In the same motion, she squeezed the trigger of her gun. Her shot missed, slamming into the wooden door frame. But it was successful in one way. Both men took cover, ducking back into the hall.

Garrett didn't let them get far. Still on his side, still bleeding, he fired.

He didn't miss.

His bullet smacked into the larger gunman's right shoulder. The second shot succeeded as well, striking the man's hand and sending his weapon flying through the air.

Garrett didn't stop there. With their baby crying and Lexie yelling for him to be careful, he scrambled across the room, putting himself in the direct line of fire. Lexie couldn't believe what he was doing. He was going to get himself killed. He was going to die.

Unless she did something.

Lexie fired. So did Garrett. She wasn't sure whose bullet succeeded, but one of the shots took out the second gunman. No flesh wound this time; it was a direct hit to the head. The guy crumpled in a heap, his gun dropping on the floor.

"Don't move," Lexie told the injured man when he started to reach for the weapon.

He didn't listen, but instead of grabbing the gun, he dived at her. Tackling her. His momentum slammed Lexie into the wall. He might be injured, but he had the advantage because of his sheer size.

Amid the frantic cries of their baby, she heard Garrett scramble across the room to help her. She needed it. Lexie tried to bring up her fist to punch the guy, but he elbowed her hand aside.

And went after her gun.

She held on and managed to bite him. She sank her teeth into his knuckles, but he didn't give up. Using his weight to hold her down, he tried to wrench the gun from her.

Then just like that, he stopped.

"Move and you die," she heard Garrett say.

Hardly able to breathe under the heavy body weight, Lexie clawed her way out from the beneath the hulking man and saw that Garrett had his gun pressed to the back of his head.

"Please give me an excuse to fire," Garrett said, his voice laced with rage. "*Any* excuse. Because I really, really want to hurt you."

Lexie didn't doubt that. Neither did the man. In an act of surrender, he dropped to his stomach and flattened his arms and hands on the floor. Garrett stood over him with his Glock, ready to take him out if necessary.

Lexie stayed put, mainly because her feet seemed glued in place, but she checked Garrett's wound. His left arm was bleeding and he obviously needed medical attention. She turned to grab the cell phone so she could make sure an ambulance was on the way, but detected movement out of the corner of her eye.

Movement near the bassinet.

There was someone standing over the baby, and the person had a gun.

"I trust you won't do anything stupid," the woman said. She stepped from the shadows. "The stakes are so high. And they just got a lot higher."

IT WAS CHAOS.

The baby was crying. The goon on the floor was wounded, but with the arrival of his boss, he was chuckling and trying to get to his feet. Garrett's head was pounding, and though he didn't think his wound was serious, it was throbbing and bleeding like crazy. Unfortunately, he couldn't deal with any of those things.

Because of Dr. Linnay Blake.

She was by the bassinet, and her gun was way too close to the baby.

Worse, Garrett heard something. Some movement

in the hall. "Did you bring Irving Kent with you?" he asked the doctor, and tried to brace himself for a second wave of attack.

"No. I found you all on my own," Linnay happily informed him. "With the tracking device I planted on your car when you went to meet Dr. Darnell at the mission. I'm so glad he called me to come to that meeting. If he hadn't, I might have never found you."

"Lucky us," Garrett mumbled. He volleyed glances between Linnay and the doorway.

"Lucky me," Linnay countered. "But I did have to wait a while before making this visit. I had to tie up some other loose ends. It just wasn't a good idea to have evidence lying around for others to find. But now that I've taken care of that, you're priority on my list of things to do."

Garrett didn't have to wait long to see what he was up against. Yet another gunman stepped into view. The woman had certainly come prepared.

But prepared for what?

"I can't let you take the baby," Garrett informed her. He made a quick check to ensure that Lexie was okay. She was, for the most part. She hadn't been visibly injured, but he knew she was terrified for their child.

"I don't think you're in any shape to bargain. You've got about a pint of blood dripping down your arm, and you have no leverage whatsoever. Why? Because if you want your baby to live, then the two of you have to die. I can't leave any witnesses."

"There's Irving Kent, the nanny and the two guards being held at headquarters," Lexie pointed out. "That's a lot of witnesses."

"None of them can trace anything back to me, and when I'm done here, everything will be pinned on Irving Kent." She checked her watch and glanced at the gunman who'd just gotten off the floor. "Finish this mess," she ordered. "I'm leaving for the airport."

Dr. Blake scooped up the crying baby and headed for the door. Garrett nearly launched himself at her, but he quickly realized he had to do something or Lexie would be killed. The third gunman had already aimed his Sig-Sauer at her. Worse, Lexie had her attention focused on the baby and didn't seem to realize the danger.

"Get down," Garrett yelled.

He couldn't wait to see if she complied; he had to keep his attention on the gunmen. He also had to wait until Dr. Blake was out of the way, for he couldn't risk hurting the baby. Apparently the thugs felt the same, because both held off until the doctor disappeared into the hall.

The reprieve didn't last long. The gunman in the doorway fired at him. Garrett dropped to the floor, and the bullet whizzed past his head. The next shot, however, hit his gun, which flew from his hand.

Out of the corner of his eye, Garrett saw Lexie deliver one of those martial arts kicks to the wounded gunman. Garrett only prayed she could hold her own and stay out of the path of the bullets. Because the gunman fired again.

And again.

It was pure luck and some fancy moves that kept Garrett from being hit. But he wasn't worried about himself. He was worried about Lexie and the baby. Lexie and he had to take care of these two goons so they could stop Linnay Blake from getting to the airport. If she managed to get on that jet, they might never see their daughter again.

Acting fast, Garrett dived at the man, and they both went sprawling. Garrett managed to grab the guy's wrist, and pounded it hard against the floor. Over and over again until the gun dropped.

He could hear the sounds of Lexie fighting for her life. He could still hear the faint sounds of his baby crying. Garrett used both to give him a second slam of adrenaline. He aimed his fist at the guy's jaw and punched. And punched. And punched.

He didn't stop there. He retrieved the gunman's Sig-Sauer and went after the thug who had Lexie in a chokehold. She kneed the guy in the groin at the exact second that Garrett bashed the butt of his gun against the back of their attacker's head.

It didn't kill him, but it knocked him out cold.

"Let's go," Lexie said, without even pausing for breath. She retrieved her gun, and Garrett was one step ahead of her when they raced out of the room.

"Which way?" she asked. "The garage or the front?"

"The front," Garrett immediately answered. Probably the driveway. And he prayed he was right.

Because it was a high probability that they had one chance—just one—to rescue their child.

JUST AHEAD OF HER, Garrett jerked open the front door, and they sprinted outside. The muggy night breeze was smothering, and it didn't help that she couldn't seem to catch her breath.

Lexie quickly tried to get her bearings. She could hear police sirens in the distance. Not nearly close enough.

It was dark, and someone had obviously shot out the streetlights. But the hunter's moon allowed Lexie to spot the dark-colored car in the driveway.

The headlights were off.

There were heavily tinted windows.

And the engine was running.

The sound she heard next turned her mouth to dust. The driver hit the accelerator, gunning the engine. It was almost certainly Linnay Blake, since she'd seemingly run out of hired thugs. Still, the doctor wouldn't need a hired gun if she managed to get to the airport. She'd be home free, able to fly out of the country.

Lexie didn't intend for that to happen.

She couldn't lose their baby. Not again. And she couldn't lose Garrett, who needed to get to a hospital. That meant they had to end this here and now.

Neither Garrett nor she said anything. They simply started to run toward the car. Both of them. Fast. As if their lives depended on it.

Because they did.

The vehicle shot out of the driveway, and the driver floored the accelerator. That didn't stop Garrett or her. They launched themselves onto the hood of the car. Lexie could see her baby strapped into an infant carrier in the back seat. And she could see the driver.

It was definitely Linnay Blake.

With one hand on the wheel, the doctor used her other hand to aim her weapon—just as Garrett started smashing his gun on the windshield. The doctor jerked the steering wheel to the left—probably an attempt to throw them off. It almost worked. Lexie grabbed a windshield wiper and held on, using her own gun to help Garrett bash through the glass.

Cursing and shouting, Linnay tried to take aim again. But with one final slam of his gun, Garrett made an opening in the glass. Lightning fast, he shoved his fist toward her, knocking her gun away. Once that was done, he clamped his hand around her throat.

Struggling, the woman slammed on the brakes and took her hands from the steering wheel to claw at his arm.

Though the car was still moving, Lexie slid off the hood and grabbed the handle of the passenger door.

It was locked.

She could hear her baby crying and the struggle

going on between Linnay and Garrett as she grabbed the handle of the back door. It opened. She leaped in and scrambled across the seat to the strapped-in carrier, shielding her baby's body with her own.

And not a second too soon.

Linnay gunned the engine again. The car lurched forward, but only went a few yards before it slammed into a streetlight. The airbag inflated. Glass flew; Lexie could feel it pelting her back. Once it stopped, she reeled around in the seat, terrified of what she might see.

Garrett had to be all right.

Lexie began to bargain with the powers that be to save him.

She saw Linnay first. Unconscious, she was slumped against the airbag. But Lexie couldn't see Garrett. She couldn't hear him. She could only hear the baby's cries and the police sirens.

With her hands shaking, Lexie picked up her daughter and tried to soothe her with murmurs and whispers that were more frantic than comforting. Still, the baby responded. She grew quiet almost immediately. Not Lexie, though. She started to call out for Garrett.

She jumped from the car, holding the baby against her. Praying. Mercy, she was praying. And she saw him. Not on the car. But on the ground. Lying there.

Not moving.

Somehow, she got to him, though the fear created a crushing pain in her chest.

"Garrett!"

He still didn't move. Frantically, she called out his name again, and she could feel hot tears spill down her cheeks.

Lexie dropped to her knees, just as the police cruisers rounded the corner. Their headlights allowed her to see the nicks and cuts on his face. She also saw the blood from the gunshot wound on his arm.

"Don't you dare die," she said, her voice hoarse and raw. "You can't die. Because I love you."

Chapter Twenty

"Watch your step," Lexie reminded him.

Garrett did, mainly because he didn't want to fall walking up the stairs to his own house. He also didn't want to add more injuries to his present ones, especially since it'd taken two days to convince the doctors to discharge him from the hospital. He had no plans to go back there anytime soon.

"Just lean on me," Lexie added.

Oh, he did. He really didn't need her to support his weight, but there was something comforting about having her arms wrapped around him.

"Is it my imagination or are you enjoying this TLC?" Brayden asked. He was behind them, carrying the baby. Garrett didn't have to see his brother to know he was smirking.

Garrett glanced over his shoulder and flashed him a grin. Which hurt a little, because his jaw was still bruised. He wasn't sure how it'd gotten that way.

Maybe the fistfight with the gunman. Or maybe from the car crash. However, it was a small price to pay to have Lexie and their baby safe. Ditto for the hole the bullet had left in his arm. A clear pass through. Soon, the only reminder would be a scar.

"I had your garage fixed," Brayden pointed out.

And someone had cleaned the place, Garrett noted when they went inside. Maybe Lexie, though she'd spent most of her time at the hospital with him.

Once she had him seated on the sofa, she took the baby from Brayden. "I have to change her diaper. I won't be long." She gave Garrett a quick kiss on the cheek.

Brayden lifted an eyebrow.

Garrett lifted his.

They shared a smile.

However, the smile was short-lived, because Garrett knew they had some things to discuss. Important things he didn't want to talk about in front of Lexie. Though she no doubt already knew. Garrett just didn't want her to have to relive any of what'd happened.

"You're sure Linnay Blake doesn't have any more hired guns lurking out there who might want to pay us a visit?" he asked Brayden.

"No way. I personally went through her records, and we got all of her employees. Most had minor roles. Like Irving Kent. And the hired gun who dressed up like a cop. I don't believe even Dr. Darnell had the entire picture. Linnay Blake was the one in charge, and she made millions off the illegal adoptions. Fortunately, all of her former employees are willing to testify to the bits of info they do have. Those bits all add up to a lot of evidence we can use to put her away for life without the possibility of parole."

Good. That was a start, but Garrett wanted more. "What about Billy Avery? Is he holding a grudge against Lexie?"

Brayden shook his head. "In fact, he seems relieved to be exonerated from the baby stealing charges. Honor among thieves and all that. Avery apparently didn't have a problem extorting money and intimidating witnesses, but even he draws the line at kidnapping babies."

That was something, at least. Garrett darn sure didn't want to tangle with Billy Avery. Not after what they'd been through. "So, we're in the clear?"

"Almost." Brayden took a deep breath. "You still have to do some reports at headquarters."

Yeah. That. "And there's likely the butt-chewing I'll get from Lieutenant Dillard. It'll probably lead to my dismissal. I'll just resign and make things easier for everyone."

"Don't be too hasty. You're one of the best cops at headquarters, and none of us plans to let you get away." Brayden stood and extracted something from his jacket pocket. Two items he tossed to Garrett.

A piece of paper and his badge.

They landed in his lap and lay there. The badge, a symbol of what he'd thought was the most important thing in his life. He checked the paper. It was a lab slip with the DNA test results. The baby was Lexie's and his. Not that Garrett needed a test to confirm it.

"No more administrative leave," Brayden clarified. "Full reinstatement, after you've recovered, of course."

Garrett had to clear the lump from his throat. "Dillard's okay with this?"

"It was his suggestion." Brayden stared down at him. "You have no idea just how good you are, do you?" He didn't wait for a response. Not that Garrett would have known what to say. In addition to the lump in his throat, he was speechless. "That's my fault. I should have told you just what you mean to the department. And to me."

Hell, that lump got worse. "I'm good at bashing in doors," Garrett reminded him.

"You're good, *period.* You're the first cop I call into a situation when all hell's breaking loose. You don't always play by the rules, but then neither do the bad guys. Case in point—if you'd listened to me, if you'd followed the rules, you might not have gotten your daughter back."

Garrett took a moment to compose himself. "Thank you."

"Thank *you*," Brayden declared. His posture changed when they heard Lexie returning.

Garrett understood his brother's nonverbal cues. Their heart to heart, soul-baring conversation was just for them. Still, Garrett was well aware that he'd just received a precious gift—affirmation from a cop whom he respected and admired above all others. He would carry it and the badge with him.

"Lieutenant Dillard will thank you, too, when you're back on duty," Brayden continued, his voice lighter now. "Heck, you'll even get a commendation for collaring Linnay Blake and putting an end to this illegal adoption ring."

"That's wonderful," Lexie said.

Garrett glanced up and saw her in the doorway. She looked great. Rested. Happy.

Hot.

She had on one of those cottony dresses that skimmed her body. A dress he intended to remove once they were alone and the baby was napping.

And speaking of the baby, Lexie had her cradled against her. A squirming baby who was making cooing and gurgling sounds. He put the badge on the end table so he could reach for his daughter. Lexie accommodated him, depositing the child into his waiting arms, and then she sat next to him.

Brayden tipped his head toward the badge. "You used to break out in hives if you weren't wearing it."

"I'll put it on later. All those edges might scratch the baby."

His daughter must have approved of that decision because she looked up at him and cooed. It was a rather amazing sound. And obviously an indication that she was a genius.

"According to one of the parenting books I've been reading, you're supposed to coo and gurgle back when she does that," Lexie told him. "It encourages speech development."

"Maybe." Garrett tried a coo, but it sounded a little scary. "But it won't do much for my bad boy image."

"Neither will changing diapers," Lexie added with grin.

Brayden grinned as well. "I suppose a lot of things will change." He looked at Lexie. "I don't know if you plan to go back to being a bodyguard anytime soon, but if you're interested, I can ask around."

She shook her head. "I have some money set aside so I can afford to take time off to be with the baby. Besides, being a bodyguard has lost some of its luster." She pointed to the box of files that had been brought over from the safe house. "Dr. Darnell and Dr. Blake ruined a lot of lives. I might be able to help. We have those records. It wouldn't be official because of how the records were obtained, but I can try to locate the birth mothers and let them know what happened to their children."

Garrett nodded. It was a good cause, and while he was still on medical leave, he could help her. But more than that, he was simply looking forward to spending time with Lexie and their baby.

Brayden checked his watch. "I figure you've got less than fifteen minutes before the family arrives. I'll wait for them on the porch and go over the rules."

"Rules?" Lexie questioned.

"Trust me, you'll want rules—especially since the family has had two days to plan this little get-to-gether. That's what you get for Garrett not wanting the whole O'Malley clan to visit him in the hospital."

"I didn't want to introduce them to Lexie and the baby until I was home," Garrett explained.

"Can't say I blame you. Still, there's a definite need for rules. I'll let them know that they can't grill Lexie about your intentions toward her. They can't suggest baby names. And finally, they can't stay long. I'm sure both of you are eager to get some…rest."

That last part sounded a little raunchy, but Garrett conceded that it might be his own interpretation. During the past two days, he'd had a lot of hot, lurid thoughts about Lexie, and none of them involved rest. Just clothing removal.

"Speaking of baby names," Lexie murmured, "I was thinking about Erin."

"Erin O'Malley," Brayden and Garrett said in **unison.**

Lexie glanced at them. "Something wrong with that?"

"Nope," Brayden answered. He stood. "It's Irish. I'm sure it'll meet with family approval." He excused himself and went outside onto the porch, closing the door behind him.

Garrett looked at Lexie. She was nibbling on her bottom lip. He leaned over and kissed her. And then did some nibbling of his own.

Her participation was good, but he knew she could do a lot better. "You're nervous about meeting my family."

"You bet I am. I don't know what they'll think of me for running out on you."

Oh, this was easy. "They'll love you. *I* love you."

There. He'd said it. And it was surprisingly painless. In fact, he rather liked the way it sounded. Liked even better the way it made him feel. So he said it again.

"I love you, Lexie."

The lip nibbling stopped, and she made a little sound in her throat. He was pretty sure it was a sound of happiness. His first clue was when she practically launched herself into his arms, and he ended up holding both Lexie and Erin.

It was heaven.

Well, almost.

Then Lexie made it heaven.

"I love you, too, Garrett."

He'd heard her say it before. While he lay on the ground bleeding. But he had a powerful reaction, hearing it again. His heart actually did a little flutter. Not very manly or bad boy of him. However, he was hoping for a lot more flutters in their future.

Especially once he got her out of that dress.

She put her mouth to his and whispered against his lips. "How could I not love a man who bashes down doors and windows to save our baby and me?"

"You bashed stuff, too."

"Yes. I think that's why we're a good match."

He was pleased to hear that, because he felt the same way.

"Marry me, Lexie." He saw the surprise on her face and panicked a little. "I'm afraid to make that a question. I need you to say yes."

The surprised look turned into a smile. "I need to say yes as well."

He'd expected to feel happiness. He did. But he also felt relief. "You mean that?"

She put her mouth to his once again. "There's no place I'd rather be than right here with you."

"We can do better than that. How about in my bed?"

"That, too. But I think for the next month or so, we'll have to settle for quickies. Because of the baby. She's not much for long naps."

"I'm good at quickies."

"I'll bet you are." She kissed him back and managed to leave him wanting more. A lot more.

However, Garrett put their passion on hold a little longer so he could reach in his pocket for a small black box, obviously designed to hold jewelry.

Lexie's eyes widened. "When did you find time to get a ring?"

"I didn't. I'd planned to pick out your engagement ring tomorrow." He used his thumb to flip open the box.

She opened her mouth. Closed it. And just like that, tears sprang to her eyes.

"Oh, man," Garrett grumbled. "I made you cry."

"They're good tears," she promised. She reached into the box and took out the delicate gold and diamond necklace. The last gift her father had given her. The one she'd pawned to survive. "How did you find it?"

"I hired a P.I. to search every pawnshop in the city and surrounding area." Since her hands were trembling, Garrett helped her put it around her neck.

For a moment he thought it'd been a mistake to give it to her on a day already filled to the brim with emotion. But when she eased back and they faced each other again, he knew he'd made the right decision.

"Thank you." And she kissed him. It was French and hot. Well, as French and hot as it could be, considering he still had the baby in his arms.

"Hold that thought," he whispered when he heard voices outside. "We'll do something about it as soon Erin's down for a nap and my family leaves."

That hot, sultry look in her eyes vanished, replaced by nervousness. That wouldn't last long. His family would quickly put her at ease.

He stood, drawing both Lexie and Erin to him. Definitely heaven.

They went to the window and looked out. His parents, sister, brother-in-law, Brayden's wife and their three kids were making their way onto the porch. All were smiling, and some—especially his mom—looked as nervous as Lexie.

"You were right," Lexie mumbled. "They have a Bundt cake and lots of pink stuff."

They did indeed. Pink balloons. Pink roses. Pink gift bags with matching ribbon. And there was an enormous pink-wrapped package in the shape of a bear. His nephew was carrying a pink plastic badge and a pink bubble gum cigar.

"Remember that part about them loving you," Garrett reminded her.

"And remember that part about *me* loving *you*," she reminded him.

"Always."

He'd gone through life knowing that something was missing. Something he couldn't quite put his finger on. But he certainly knew what it was now.

Lexie and his daughter.

They were the parts of the puzzle that made everything complete. They made *him* complete.

Garrett pulled them both into his arms and waited for his family to welcome—and fall in love with—the newest O'Malleys.

* * * * *

Don't miss Delores Fossen's next
romantic suspense book,
COVERT CONCEPTION,
on sale in October 2006,
only from Harlequin Intrigue!

SAVE UP TO $30! SIGN UP TODAY!

INSIDE *Romance*

The complete guide to your favorite Harlequin®, Silhouette® and Love Inspired® books.

✓ Newsletter ABSOLUTELY FREE! No purchase necessary.

✓ Valuable coupons for future purchases of Harlequin, Silhouette and Love Inspired books in every issue!

✓ Special excerpts & previews in each issue. Learn about all the hottest titles before they arrive in stores.

✓ No hassle—mailed directly to your door!

✓ Comes complete with a handy shopping checklist so you won't miss out on any titles.

- -

SIGN ME UP TO RECEIVE INSIDE ROMANCE ABSOLUTELY FREE
(Please print clearly)

Name _____

Address _____

City/Town _____ State/Province _____ Zip/Postal Code _____

(098 KKM EJL9)

Please mail this form to:
In the U.S.A.: Inside Romance, P.O. Box 9057, Buffalo, NY 14269-9057
In Canada: Inside Romance, P.O. Box 622, Fort Erie, ON L2A 5X3
OR visit http://www.eHarlequin.com/insideromance

IRNBPA06R   ® and ™ are trademarks owned and used by the trademark owner and/or its licensee.

HARLEQUIN® Romance

A family saga begins to unravel when the doors to the Bella Lucia Restaurant Empire are opened...

The Brides of Bella Lucia

A family torn apart by secrets, reunited by marriage

AUGUST 2006

Meet Rachel Valentine, in
HAVING THE FRENCHMAN'S BABY
by Rebecca Winters

Find out what happens when a night of passion is followed by a shocking revelation and an unexpected pregnancy!

SEPTEMBER 2006

The Valentine family saga continues with
THE REBEL PRINCE by Raye Morgan

HRBB0706BW

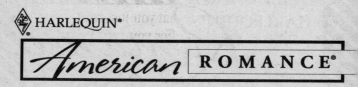

If you enjoyed what you just read,
then we've got an offer you can't resist!

Take 2 bestselling love stories FREE!

Plus get a FREE surprise gift!

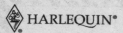
INTRIGUE

COMING NEXT MONTH